HIGH-WATER CARGO

Whittlesey House

McGraw-Hill Book Company, Inc.   New York   London   Toronto

HIGH-WATER CARGO

by **EDITH M. DORIAN**

illustrated by **FORREST ORR**

HIGH-WATER CARGO

Published by Whittlesey House

A division of the McGraw-Hill Book Company, Inc.

PRINTED IN THE UNITED STATES OF AMERICA

For *GRANDMOTHER*
and *NANCY*
and the two *DONS*

CONTENTS

CHAPTER ONE

The Lockkeeper's Son

DIRCK VAN ARSDALEN was heading for the back door, hoe in hand, when his mother ran into the kitchen to toss him a quart pail and a cheerful good morning simultaneously.

"Bring back strawberries for pie, son. And don't forget the horn will blow for breakfast soon."

Dirck smiled at her and strolled out the door. He wasn't fond enough of hoeing the garden patch on the canal bank to feel like hurrying, and the thought of picking strawberries didn't brighten the morning any. Making his way down the path through his mother's neat herb garden, he threw a glance in the direction of the house across the street. Maybe Maddy Brandt would be out, and he could bribe her into doing the picking. Yes, there she was, scrubbing the last stone step on their front stoop with the traditional thoroughness of her Dutch ancestors.

Regular angel she looked when the sun made a halo of her blond curls that way. Dirck sniffed. Maddy used to be all right enough when she was little. After he mended the broken doll she was crying over in the corner of the garden one day, she got to be pretty useful helping him grub weeds and fetching things he forgot. Of course, she was always underfoot, but he got so used to her around he didn't even bother to correct people who thought she was his little sister.

Lately though, she was different, not half as useful, and she could tease like sin. Sometimes nowadays he wished she was his sister; then he'd drub some manners into her, that was sure. Right now, however, diplomacy was indicated. Dirck whistled and waved his pail.

"Strawberries, Maddy," he called. "Come on and pick while I hoe the corn patch. Take you fishing next time if you do."

Maddy put her head on one side and considered.

"Honest?" she demanded. "Even if I talk?"

Dirck swallowed uncomfortably.

"Sure," he agreed, "though why you have to be always talking beats me. Scare the fish right off the hook, that's what you do, and then wonder why we haven't caught any for supper!"

Maddy grinned cheerfully and came across Burnet Street to grab the pail and run ahead of him down the path across the footbridge to the berry patch. She began to pick skillfully, her hands darting among the leaves like hummingbirds, and though she didn't say a word, Dirck could see her lips moving.

From his stand in the corn, the boy saw that his lock-keeper father had the outlet open and that the barges, tied up for the night, were on the move. My, but the Raritan was black with rafts this morning, a lot of them waiting to be floated into the canal and start the long tow to the Delaware River. Mules were already lined up on the towpath, ready to haul the loads along. Dirck looked over at Maddy.

"You sick?" he demanded. "A body'd think so the way you're muttering to yourself."

Frowning in concentration, Maddy didn't bother to answer. Then suddenly she clapped her hands and shouted excitedly.

"A hundred and eleven! Dirck Van Arsdalen, there are a hundred and eleven barges in those tows floating out the canal right this minute. If I were a shareholder in the canal company, I'd be rich enough to go over to the steamboat landing and ride on the *Antelope* all the way to New York. Oh, Dirck, do you suppose I'll ever get to go?"

Her face was so wistful the boy couldn't help reassuring her.

"Someday, Maddy. We'll both go. Maybe it won't be for a long time, but we'll go—after I've finished Rutgers when I'm an engineer, building bridges and canals myself."

The girl's face sobered.

"But, Dirck," she objected, "your father still doesn't want you to go to Rutgers. He was talking to my father last night. With my own ears I heard him say you'd be flying in the face of Providence not to be a tinker when your hands can mend anything. He says wanting to go to Rutgers is just a crazy boy's notion you'll outgrow. But you won't, Dirck, will you? Promise me you won't. I'll hate you always, Dirck Van Arsdalen, if you stay just Dirck the Tinker when you could be Dirck the Engineer!"

And thrusting the pail of strawberries into his hand, Maddy was gone in a whirl of skirts.

Slowly Dirck walked back to the house for breakfast. Maddy was getting to be impossible. What need did she have to fly at him like that? She knew he wasn't going to let a nickname shape his whole life. What if he was called Tinker? His brother Pieter used to be called Farmer, and now he was going to be a minister. Dirck clamped his square Dutch jaw. He'd be an engineer yet. He'd make his father see how important it was to study mathematics at Rutgers College soon.

There isn't any better father than mine, Dirck thought loyally, but sometimes he just can't seem to understand.

To Jacobus Van Arsdalen college was meant for students of theology like his son Pieter. It was as simple as A B C. He even stretched a point and conceded that schoolmasters might find college learning useful. But Dirck had no bent for either calling; he was a typical Van Arsdalen.

Until Pieter came along, the big Van Arsdalen family Bible showed an unbroken record of carpenters and blacksmiths, plain God-fearing men with no taste for book learning. Had his older son suddenly wanted to run for president, the lockkeeper wouldn't have been more astonished than to have him ask permission to enter the seminary at Rutgers. At first he had thought that Pieter wanted to be parish *voorleser,* lay reader and comforter of the sick. It had taken time to grasp his full ambition to be ordained and to turn the first bewilderment into happy pride.

But if the Lord had called Pieter to His service, He had just as surely given Dirck hands even more skillful with tools than the generations of Van Arsdalens behind him. When you were cut out to be a tinker, you might as well accept the fact and be the best tinker possible. Rutgers didn't teach tinkering or any nonsense like engineering either. It taught theology and languages and higher mathematics and natural philosophy.

Dirck's face set stubbornly as he thought of his father's arguments. He knew the expenses of the seminary were a heavy burden on his family, though Pieter earned whatever he could in his spare time. But he wasn't asking for money himself; he'd earn it somehow. All he wanted now was permission to try. Building bridges took more than the arithmetic he'd learned from Schoolmaster Vanderveer; he needed at least two years in college to make an apprenticeship in an engineer's office worth while.

Somehow he had to convince his father that being a tinker wasn't enough, that being an engineer mattered more than anything else in the world. He'd do it somehow. Maddy knew that as well as he did. There wasn't any reason for her to get all riled up that way.

Back in the kitchen, Dirck dismissed the whole bothersome problem and ate his breakfast with a good appetite, stowing away dried-apple coffee cake and homemade sausage as though he might not eat again for a week.

"That's a good pailful of berries, Dirck. You couldn't have had much time to finish your hoeing. I didn't mean to hold up your chores."

His mother, pretty and plump and rosy, smiled at him over her cup of chocolate, and Dirck grinned back.

"Maddy picked 'em," he admitted. "She didn't have anything else to do."

"So Maddy picked them, did she?" Mrs. Van Arsdalen tried to look severe. "I guessed as much. It's time, young man, you did your own picking. Maddy has been spoiling you for years. We can't be having you ruined just because your fingers had a knack for mending broken dolls."

Dirck snorted. "You needn't worry any about Maddy. I had to promise to take her fishing to get her to do it. Anyway, she's getting too big for her boots. What makes her act so contrary, Mother, quarreling and ordering you around when all you want is a little peace?"

"Just growing pains, Dirck," his mother answered quietly. "You've been ordering Maddy around for years. I know you're sixteen, but Maddy isn't toddling any more; she's fourteen and maybe she thinks it's her turn." She changed the subject briskly. "If you've finished your breakfast, you'd better carry a mug of chocolate and some bread and cheese down to your father. It doesn't look as though he can leave the lock."

Dirck nodded agreement. "Maddy counted a hundred and eleven coal barges going down the canal, and there were plenty moving in. Father likely won't be back till noon. Probably he has jobs for me. Anyway, I'd better be off to see."

And with a parting hug that nearly capsized the mug of chocolate down his mother's back, Dirck was gone, cheerfully whistling "Yankee Doodle" off key.

CHAPTER TWO

Danger on the Wharf

DOWN AT THE outlet lock, barges were moving in a slow parade, their crews exchanging upriver gossip as they floated along, all of them shouting a greeting to the big Dutchman smoking his pipe on the bank. Dirck watched his father admiringly. He knew that even the roughest bargeman had small hankering for a tussle with the New Brunswick lockkeeper. Jacobus was a patient man, slow to anger, but he was six feet four of solid brawn with tough muscles and iron fists. Plenty of rivermen had learned from experience that he could use them to good effect. Seeing his son now, he waved his pipe, motioning the boy on with a gesture that set Dirck trotting.

"Mother sent some food, Father," he called as soon as he was close enough to be heard over the din at the lock. "She was afraid you couldn't leave for a while."

"No more I can, leastways not until this tangle goes through safely, say in a couple of hours' time. I'll eat when the lull comes, and you can take over. There'll be no trouble you can't handle once these Hoboken crews get by."

Mr. Van Arsdalen bit into his bread and cheese with gusto and smiled slowly at his son.

"Food almost made me forget what I wanted you for. Ryle Cornel is looking for someone to take a couple of mules down to the smithy. You'll have plenty of time before I need you here, so be off with you. Ryle's got them tied up by the big sycamore tree farther down the bank. Perhaps you can get through to the Square before steamboat time; it'll be easier."

Dirck nodded and raced away. "It'd be easier all right," he muttered, but by the time he had reached the mules and untethered them, he was already too late. The daily battle of the rival boatlines had begun. Wheels were rumbling into Burnet Street from Albany, and galloping hoofs were scattering foot passengers to the comparative safety of the narrow plank sidewalks. Dirck took one look northward and tethered Ryle's mules again well down the bank. If anything went careening off the road, he had no intention of letting the tow mules come out of the melee with a couple of broken legs.

From where he stood, he could see a blur of plumes on gaily caparisoned horses and feel the staccato blasts of the heralds' horns against his ears. Below him scattered touters were yelling themselves hoarse soliciting passengers for the *John Neilson* or the *Antelope*. People were pouring down into Burnet Street, heading for the huge wharf that spread horizontally along the river about a block beyond the outlet from the canal. Then the omnibuses of both boatlines tore by, racing each other furiously, their drivers standing braced, shouting defiance at each other and the

16

world. Thick, choking clouds of red dust swirled high and set folks to coughing hectically.

Dirck found that he had been holding his breath in excitement. Quickly he calculated his chances of leading the mules through the motley collection of carts and people crowding along in the wake of the swaying omnibuses. A halter rope in either hand, he moved cautiously forward across the stream. Wheelbarrows filled with luggage barked his shins. Wagoners shouted angrily, impatient at having to haul in their horses to let the boy struggle by. Even the mules showed signs of nerves. But once over Burnet Street, Dirck prodded them in a trot to Commerce Square. With a bit of luck they'd have to wait their turn, and he'd still have a chance to slip down to the wharf before the boats cast off.

His luck held. The smith was busy; Dirck counted four horses ahead of his mules. Usually he was content to stay, glad to lend a hand at the anvil and hammer out a shoe, but today he couldn't stand still. His feet were itching to be off; his ears were tuned to the roar of escaping steam down by the river.

"I'll be back for them soon, Tom," he called and sped out the door in a dash for the landing.

Running over the fields in a short cut, he soon began to wriggle his way through the mob on the wharf. Both boats, their colors flying, had their steam up ready to cast off; patrons of each line leaned over the railings exchanging cigars and jokes and laying wagers on the running time into New York. Wagons of every description swarmed on the wharf, their horses rearing and kicking in inextricable confusion, to the imminent hazard of anyone unlucky enough to be pushed too close.

Dirck ducked a pawing hoof and wedged himself against a piling where he had a fair view just as a late passenger's carriage turned onto the wharf, its elderly coachman pleading loudly for right of way. Good-naturedly people pushed back, and Dirck caught a glimpse of Nicholas Ten Eyck, his hand on his carriage door, ready to spring out.

Then everything happened at once. A dray horse, momentarily frightened by the *Antelope's* blasting whistle, reared frantically backward, ramming the heavy cart behind him into Ten Eyck's right front wheel. Its axle snapped with a crack that sent the carriage pair into a mad plunge, tilting the carriage sharply and hurling the coachman clear of his box.

Instinctively Dirck sprang forward. Jumping upward, he seized the terrified bays by their bridle reins and hung on grimly. His arms felt wrenched half out of their sockets, but the horses were quieting, their flanks quivering now and their heads beginning to droop. From the tail of his eye, Dirck saw Mr. Ten Eyck tear the door open and run to his coachman's side.

"Tim, Tim!" he called urgently. "Are you all right? Can you talk to me, man?"

Slowly the old colored man opened his eyes. He looked dazed, but he smiled at his master reassuringly.

"I'm all right, Mr. Nicholas; 'deed I am; just kinda sore, sir. You better catch dat steamboat, Mr. Nicholas; it'll sho go off without you."

Up in the pilothouse of the *John Neilson,* Captain Frazee was growing impatient. In spite of the excitement ashore, the *Antelope* was casting off, her safety valves lifting under a heavy head of steam. And between him and Captain Van Wickel of the *Antelope* there was little good will lost. Nicholas Ten Eyck or no Nicholas Ten Eyck, Captain Frazee did not intend to let the *Antelope* show him her heels on the run, not even if he had to crowd her into the bank to beat her. His hand tugged sharply at his whistle.

Below on the wharf, Mr. Ten Eyck glanced briefly at the steamboat, shook his head firmly, and turned back to his protesting coachman.

"Hush, Tim. I'm not going, man. Tomorrow or the next day will do as well. Stay still now while I go thank the boy who jumped for the horses."

And with a pat on Tim's shoulder, Mr. Ten Eyck headed promptly for Dirck.

"That was quick work, young fellow," he said. "You probably saved Tim—and half a dozen others—a bad trampling. I'm mighty grateful to you, and I certainly hope you didn't get hurt yourself."

"Not a chance, sir," Dirck smiled. "Glad I was handy. These are beautiful horses, sir. Your coachman must take wonderful care of them; they trust people. It helped quiet them faster."

Mr. Ten Eyck laughed. "Oh, Tim treats them like children," he said. "He'll kill them with kindness yet." He eyed the bays shrewdly. "Yes, they're quiet enough now, but I don't want Tim trying to take them home. That was a nasty spill the old man took. I'll get a carriage and pack him off. You're Van Arsdalen's boy, aren't you, the one they call Tinker?"

Dirck nodded.

"Thought I recognized you. Think you could do me another favor and leave the bays in the stable at the Indian Queen? Tell Barckaloe I'll send for them later. The carriage will have to stay here in the way, I suppose, until Lyle Van Nuys can send over to mend it."

"I'll be glad to leave the bays at the Queen, sir, and the carriage, too, if you'll trust me. I can splice up that axle well enough to get her that far. A wooden peg and some rope will do as long as she doesn't carry weight."

Mr. Ten Eyck looked at the boy's confident face. What he saw pleased him.

"Go ahead," he nodded. "If you think you can, I expect you'll succeed. Tim and I will stop by the lock and leave word with your father."

"That will help, sir. He's expecting me to relieve him, but if you tell him what I'm about, he'll understand."

Dirck watched Mr. Ten Eyck go back to the old Negro and help him to his feet.

"That's the kind of a man worth working for," he murmured. "I'm glad I met him," and he bent contentedly to his task.

It took Dirck longer than he had figured on to patch the Ten Eyck carriage well enough to move it, but some tarred line and two bungs from discarded casks on the landing finally did the job. The boy inspected his handiwork critically. He wanted to be sure that wheel was not going to come off and send the carriage lurching into something on the road. There were ugly scratches now where the dray had rammed, but there were not going to be any more, not while he was responsible at least. Satisfied at last, he hitched up the bays again and started carefully back along Burnet Street toward the Indian Queen.

By the time he left the horses in the stable yard under the care of the ostler, Dirck was beginning to worry. The town clock, built into the tower of the old Dutch Church, stood at nine-thirty. After all, his father had to eat; he ought to be getting back to the lock.

Hope I don't have to chase all over this place to find Mr. Barckaloe, he thought. I want to get going.

He darted in the kitchen door and almost collided with the man he was seeking. But the innkeeper didn't even see him. He was in a colossal rage, storming around the big room, his face choleric.

"Pesky boy!" he was roaring. "I ought to be glad to see the last of him. Lazy, good-for-nothing scalawag, that's all he was. Ought to have known he wouldn't leave empty-handed."

Suddenly catching sight of Dirck standing open-mouthed, he stopped his tramping.

"Well," he growled, "what might you want, young Tinker Van Arsdalen?"

Hastily Dirck explained that Mr. Ten Eyck's bays were in the stable yard and would be called for later. The Indian Queen was obviously not a healthy spot for boys this morning. The sooner he left, the better. "That's all, sir," he said and turned hurriedly to the door.

But the innkeeper had other ideas. "Hold your horses, hold your horses, young man. I haven't finished with you. That rascally boy we had skipped in the night—with a lodger's purse in his breeches. We could use you when your father can spare you. Afternoon and early evening. Go ask him. Wages'll be a dollar a week."

Dirck stood stock-still. He could hardly credit his ears. A dollar a week! The innkeeper must be crazy. Why, with a dollar a week he'd have almost enough money for college.

Staats Barckaloe eyed him sharply. "Kinda high I know," he snorted, "but peace of mind is what I'm aiming for. Give me that, and you'll be worth it."

"I'd try, Mr. Barckaloe." Dirck nearly stammered with excitement. "I'll come if Father says it's all right. I'll be back to let you know."

He was out the door and haring for the smithy. Those mules were going to have to fly home to keep up with the wings on his heels.

CHAPTER THREE

At the Indian Queen

To DIRCK, striding along Burnet Street, New Brunswick seemed nearly empty. Heat haze, thick as fog, had stalked in over the meadows along the Raritan River, and the streets steamed. Maybe it was a good day to stay hidden indoors out of the smothering June heat, but nothing short of a broken neck would have kept him away from the Indian Queen that afternoon. The boy chuckled at the memory of his father's astonished face yesterday when he and the mules came tearing back to the lock.

"I'm not starving yet," Mr. Van Arsdalen had called drily, "leastways not enough to warrant wearing the beasts' new shoes right off their feet!"

Then, catching sight of Dirck's excited face, he had hurried over to him anxiously. "Something wrong in the town, lad? With all the noise here, I wouldn't have heard even a fire call."

But when Dirck had told his story in a pellmell rush of words, Mr. Van Arsdalen was pleased. True, he had considered the innkeeper's proposal with what seemed to his son maddening deliberation, but he had given consent quite willingly at last.

"Barckaloe is a just man. He'll treat you fairly. Give him full measure in return for his wages, son." Then he had smiled. "It's not every inn that has a tinker ready to hand. As for the wages, they're your own once you pay your mother thirty-five cents for your weekly board. I don't hold with the notion that a boy willing to work isn't free of his own money when his family can manage to spare it. And I'm glad you were quick-witted down at the landing."

Dirck recalled his father's words contentedly. He'd have plenty to tell his brother Pieter when he came home for Sunday dinner, but he wouldn't tell Pieter about saving his dollars for college. That was something best kept to himself. His mother had guessed, of course; he could tell, though she didn't say a word. Still, she knew that going to college wasn't just a crazy boy notion; she understood. Someday his father would see, too. This afternoon Dirck felt that anything might happen.

He swung into Albany Street. Whew, but it was hot! Insulated by his happiness, he had scarcely noticed how wet and sticky he was. A few more days like this and Albany Street would melt and run down the river. Pausing momentarily at the roadside, he watched the wagons and carriages rolling over the new wooden Toll Bridge into town. Someday he'd build bridges himself, bigger and stronger ones than the Toll Bridge over the Raritan, bridges of metal and stone. He straightened his shoulders and set his head before sprinting across the street to the door of the Indian Queen.

The common room of the inn was cool and shadowy after the shimmering heat outside. This was going to be a pleasant place to work even in August, Dirck thought, and the big fireplace set in one wall guaranteed more than just warm shins when winter rolled around. Cheerfully the boy sought out Mr. Barckaloe, comfortably settled in a huge armchair, his churchwarden pipe in full blast. The thunderclouds he had been wearing the day before had blown away, and he was his genial self.

To look easygoing was part of the innkeeper's stock in trade, but to underestimate his intelligence rarely paid, for he drove a shrewd bargain and was not often mistaken in his estimate of another man's character. Gentlemen with gold bricks to sell usually avoided the Indian Queen. They found the atmosphere uncongenial in spite of its owner's reputation for good humor and his knack for making people feel at home. Travelers generally stopped first because the inn was so conveniently located on the coach road between New York and Philadelphia; they came back because they liked Staats Barckaloe's hearty welcome, the comfortable beds he offered, and the food Antje Molenaer conjured up in her immaculate kitchen.

Mr. Barckaloe had been reading his paper when Dirck appeared for instructions.

"So you're here, young Tinker," he said. "Ready for work?"

"Yes, sir!" The boy's tone was so brisk that Mr. Barckaloe threw back his head and laughed.

"Well, then, be off to the kitchen. Antje's waiting for you; she's been shorthanded all day. But tell her I'll need you myself later. There'll be bags to fetch and customers to wait on after a bit."

The older man watched Dirck with considerable satisfaction as he disappeared through the kitchen door. Not a lazy bone in that boy; he'd do; he'd do fine.

Antje kept Dirck hard at it most of the afternoon. Pewter and copper had to be polished, and the shades on the new-fangled gas lamps cleaned till they glistened. Dirck had never operated any gas lamps. He studied them curiously, but they didn't look hard to light. The stacks of vegetables the kitchen maids were paring made his eyes widen though. Those pigs down behind the stable were certainly going to get too fat to waddle if they ate all the cores and peelings he had to carry out and dump in their pen. Dirck didn't particularly mind the chores, they were an old story; but he was secretly delighted when Mr. Barckaloe poked his head in the kitchen to tell Antje that her claim on the Tinker's time was up. He knew he was going to like listening to the townsmen and travelers drifting into the common room.

"Better feed him now," the innkeeper advised. "He might not get a chance at supper later. We have a sizable crowd already."

Antje smiled contentedly at Dirck's obvious pleasure in her cooking. Good food and plenty of it never did anybody harm, she was certain. What she couldn't abide was a picky, finicking appetite.

"If a body can't stomach good vittles," she told Dirck now, "he's warped somewhere. Show me a man who can't relish his food, and I'll show you a mean man. You can make it a rule never to trust one like that, young Tinker."

And nodding sagely, Mrs. Molenaer gathered up Dirck's dishes and shooed him out of the kitchen.

The common room was filling up with townsmen Dirck recognized, contentedly puffing at their pipes and talking over the news of the day. Here and there a man waved his pipe in friendly fashion at the boy as he began opening windows and shutters. The sudden influx of light chased the shadows, and a breeze, sprung up with the fading sun, helped dry glistening faces. Leaning out a window to fasten a shutter catch, Dirck could see shutters being fastened back all along Albany Street and people coming out on their stoops for a breath of air. Maddy Brandt, her hair curlier than ever from the humid heat, darted across the street toward the backdoor of the Queen. From the basket on her arm, Dirck knew she was bringing eggs to Antje Molenaer.

She's late today, he thought. It's steamboat time. Maybe she'll stay awhile to help her Aunt Antje if the crowd gets really big. He had a feeling it might do Maddy considerable good to see he had a new job.

And it was certainly reasonable to expect a crowd. Of course, many passengers from New York on their way to Philadelphia stayed right at Keyworth's Steamboat Hotel on the hill above the landing, but the fame of Antje Molenaer's cooking and Staats Barckalce's hospitality lured plenty across town to the Indian Queen. Already the first arrivals were turning out of Burnet Street, with small boys lugging their carpetbags at their heels. Dirck hurried over to the front door just as The Napoleon Company's omnibus drew up with a flourish, and passengers began piling out.

By the time he'd wedged a bag under each arm and grabbed two in each fist to follow the travelers over to Mr. Barckaloe's big desk in one corner, Dirck felt like a baggage rack. He just hoped he'd remember somehow which room each bag belonged in. It would be a fine how-de-do to mix up luggage the very first night, and one carpetbag looked exactly like another to him. He was grateful for the name tags buckled to the handles of some of them.

Keys jangling in his pocket, Dirck led the six new arrivals up to the second floor, stacked their bags in the hall temporarily, and began opening doors just as Trina, the chambermaid, appeared at the head of the back stairs, cans of hot water dangling from her wooden shoulder yoke. To sort the bags and turn their room keys over to the guests took only a few moments. Dirck lingered just long enough to be sure everyone was satisfied; then he left Trina in charge and ran downstairs again.

The man in Room 2, the one the others called Mr. Sylvester, looked interesting, he thought. Maybe he'd get a chance to wait on him when they all came down to supper. He'd like to know what that man did. He was dressed in regular business clothes just like the rest, but he'd never got all that tan sitting at a desk. He didn't talk like a farmer or a country gentleman, and he surely didn't have the gait of a sailor. It made Dirck wonder, for he had instinctively liked the decisive tone of his voice and his quick, generous smile.

He reminds me of Mr. Ten Eyck, he decided. Not that they look anything alike; it's just their manner. You know right off that they're men you can trust.

For the next half-hour Dirck was too busy showing incoming guests to their rooms to give thought to anything but the job on hand. The Queen was filling to capacity. His arms burdened with bags, he sidled like a crab around tables in the common room and men standing in talkative groups near the circular stairway. In spite of the noisy bustle of new arrivals, the place had an unhurried, hospitable atmosphere. Everyone seemed to feel it as soon as he entered the front door.

People seem comfortable and easy as soon as they get inside, Dirck noticed. Then, catching sight of himself in the mirror over the sideboard, he smiled. All but me, that is. I guess I'll keep right on being a discord till I get the rest of this luggage stowed safely. Good thing these bags are the last. If more folks come now, Trina will have to hang mattresses from the rafters. And dodging a stout gentleman in his path, he took his final load upstairs.

When he came back to the common room, the swinging door to the kitchen was in continuous motion. The trestle table close to the back wall already held its first load of steaming earthenware. Men all around the room sniffed approvingly and promptly knocked out their pipes. Staats Barckaloe motioned the boy over to help uncover soup tureens and casseroles and ladle out food as Antje Molenaer's staff took charge of orders and serving. Dirck concentrated grimly. He had no desire to pour any hot soup or steaming turkey potpie on himself or the person who had slipped quietly in beside him to cut the great loaves of crusty bread and fragrant Dutch coffee cakes.

Suspicious all of a sudden, he glanced sidewise. Those small hands working away with the big knife had begun to look oddly familiar. Yes, it was Maddy all right, almost completely lost in the folds of an enormous white apron, her curls tucked carefully under a starched lace cap. Her face looked as sober as Pastor Howe's in the pulpit Sundays, but her eyes were gleeful. Dirck knew it would take more than a crowd in the Indian Queen to awe Maddy, and the knowledge didn't comfort him any. Of course, she was only lending her aunt a hand because she had come late when the inn was crowded. Still, you never knew what she might do or say next these days. He gave her a brotherly sort of glare to forestall any of her tricks and returned his attention to soup.

But Maddy wasn't easily crushed. She began chattering something at him in an excited undertone.

"Exactly like a magpie," Dirck muttered. Just the same he cocked an ear in her direction. Maddy was always getting excited about the silliest things he ever heard of, but she picked up news the way a squirrel picked up nuts. It was generally smart to listen. This time she was giving him some of the information Trina had brought back to the kitchen from upstairs.

"And Trina says one of the first men you showed to his room is an engineer. Dirck, can you hear me all right? Trina says his name is Sylvester and that he is going to stay right here at the Queen while they do the new work on the canal. Oh, Dirck, maybe you'll wait on him. Anyway, I thought you'd want to know. That's why I told Aunt Antje I'd cut the bread: so I could get a chance to tell you. Now I've got to hurry home, but don't you dare to forget to tell me all about Mr. Sylvester if you see him later!" And with a dancing smile, Maddy vanished behind the kitchen door.

So engineering accounted for Mr. Sylvester's tanned face and hands! It had certainly paid to listen to Maddy this time. Why, I'm going to be able to watch him down at the outlet lock mornings. Maybe if I work it right, I'll even learn some of the things I want to know. Dirck began to feel less cheated over being born too late to see the Delaware and Raritan Canal built along the side of the river.

He looked expectantly around the room for a glimpse of Mr. Sylvester. He should be eating supper by this time, but he wasn't at any of the tables.

Perhaps he was invited somewhere for the evening, the boy thought disappointedly.

But no! Just then Mr. Nicholas Ten Eyck turned in at the door of the Queen with Mr. James Neilson by his side, and down the stairs, his hand outstretched to greet them, came Mr. Sylvester at last.

CHAPTER FOUR

Adam Huyler, Privateer

DIRCK ALMOST stopped breathing as Staats Barckaloe greeted the newcomers and led them across the room. A few seats were still vacant at some of the big tables, but close to the trestle where he worked, one small round table was entirely unoccupied.

"If they decide to sit by themselves, I'll start believing in Sinter Klaas again," the boy whispered to himself.

It certainly seemed unlikely, however, with half the people in the room hailing them and offering to squeeze in chairs somehow. Still, though they stopped to chat and exchange greetings, the three men apparently had their own notion and moved steadily toward that one vacant table. Dirck's pent-up steam nearly escaped in a whoop of satisfaction before he remembered where he was.

"How many years is it, Guy, since you were last in New Brunswick?" Mr. Ten Eyck demanded as they sat down. "I remember feeling pretty envious of the adventurous career you had ahead when I was just going to sit stuffily at the desk in Father's business."

Guy Sylvester smiled. "Just twenty years ago this spring. I was still serving an apprenticeship in Canvass White's office then, and he brought me down to help on the locks. I was scared to death for fear I'd blunder and he'd think I wasn't qualified for his recommendation! What a remarkable man he was: stiff as a martinet in his training, but when he sent us out to work on a problem, he never interfered. I expect he knew we'd do the job or die trying. And after his training, mighty few of us had to die!"

"I remember him well," James Neilson said. "He had a way of surmounting difficulties that you could never forget. It was a black day for your profession when he died. We could scarcely credit it down here, such a short time after he had finished the canal job. He never had a chance to see how successful the project really was. I think he'd be pleased if he could know that one of his own boys had come back to reoutfit his locks and widen his canal."

The three men eyed with interest the steaming plates the waitress set before them.

"Don't wake me up if I'm dreaming," Guy Sylvester chuckled. "This is the kind of food that has haunted my sleep for twelve months. We had a mighty bad cook in the construction camp in California. He kept body and soul together, but that's all you could claim for him. Got so we used to see food mirages out on the desert.

"And speaking of California, there was an old fellow there who hung around our camp, sat in the sun and watched us by the hour. He claimed to be a native New Brunswicker who'd come around the Horn on a steamer called the *Raritan*. He said she used to sail the river before her trip west. His name, if I remember correctly, was Freeman Vroom. Either of you ever hear of him?"

33

Both Mr. Ten Eyck and Mr. Neilson nodded promptly.

"But we thought he was at least a hundred when we were youngsters," Mr. Ten Eyck exclaimed. "He used to gather a crowd of boys around him and fill us full of tales of the early settlers; managed to get an Indian behind every bush."

"Well, he hasn't changed any," Mr. Sylvester laughed. "He's still full of stories. He says he may be ninety-two, but his memory is as good as ever. Somebody named Adam Huyler, a kind of privateer, I gather, seemed to be his favorite New Brunswick hero. Do you know about him, too, or was he just one of Vroom's tall stories?"

"Tall story, nothing," Mr. Ten Eyck snorted. "Huyler was as real as you are, even if he does sound incredible."

"Ten Eyck's your contemporary, Guy," James Neilson smiled. "He's too young to tell you about Huyler, but I was born when the man was still a local byword. Colonel John, my father, knew him well and admired him wholeheartedly. Nowadays people wonder where he buried his loot, and small boys are always ready to go digging around the bluffs along the river to look for it. But Huyler had no loot to bury. What he took—and it was plenty—he turned over to the patriot cause. That man was a navy all by himself.

"Why, let me tell you," James Neilson was warming to his story, "the redcoats found him such a thorn in their sides they actually outfitted an expedition against him."

Mr. Sylvester looked incredulous. "You sound like Vroom yourself, James. Come now, really—an expedition against one man!"

But Mr. Neilson was emphatic. "Fact, I assure you. Three hundred men, no less, sailed down the Raritan in January of 1782, with orders to destroy Huyler's whaleboats. They had nearly reached New Brunswick when a watchdog woke Peter Wyckoff. He threw himself on a horse, roused Captain Moses Guest, and spread the word from house to house. You can imagine the turmoil . . . lights flashing through the town, and every able-bodied man grabbing his gun and rushing into the streets."

"But did they destroy the whaleboats, man?" Mr. Sylvester's interest was thoroughly aroused.

Mr. Neilson nodded. "Yes, unfortunately they did. They reached the boats and fired them. Then, with Huyler's men on their track, they took to their heels, heading down Queen Street to their own boats at Town Lane. They had a running fight of it every step of the way, I can tell you. Volleys were poured into them from behind the walls of the Dutch Church, and a regular skirmish took place in front of the Agnew house on Burnet Street. They finally made their boats and sailed back to Staten Island, but not before they lost four killed and a goodly number wounded."

"Don't forget we had casualties, too, James," Mr. Ten Eyck cut in.

"Six wounded according to the records," Mr. Neilson agreed, "though none of the wounds proved fatal. What the New Brunswickers mourned, however, was the loss of Huyler's whaleboats. He was about the only one in town it didn't disturb. By February he had built a new one, rowing thirty oars, and was right back at his old tricks."

35

His listeners caught the pride James Neilson felt in his patriotic townsman.

"The man thought nothing of slipping down the river, landing way over in Flatbush, and marching three miles inland to some notorious nest of Tories, where he helped himself to silverplate and valuables. Then he'd cheerfully order the guards he had overpowered to report themselves to their commanding officer and skip with slaves and prisoners for ransom. How many enemy officers, both British and Hessian, he captured and paroled out of active service, nobody ever has known.

"No wonder you said Huyler sounded incredible, Nicholas," Guy Sylvester exclaimed. "Didn't the British ever try to follow him back upriver?"

"Their vessels were generally too heavy to follow him back up the shallow Raritan channel," Mr. Neilson answered, "but he took fearful chances every time, sometimes striking twice in the same night, even boarding British ships and carting off their captains. His men worshiped him, my father said; they'd follow him anywhere."

Those were exciting days all right, Dirck thought as he heard Mr. Neilson talking. Still, he knew he'd rather be alive right now in 1854. Maybe you couldn't be a hero fighting the Tories and the British, but he'd rather be an engineer like Mr. Sylvester than anything else in the world. Imagine going to California and maybe South America! People said that someday there'd be a canal built straight across Panama to save the long trip around the Horn.

I'd rather work on a canal like that, the boy decided, than even be an Adam Huyler.

Standing at the trestle behind them, watching the three men enjoy their dinner, Dirck grinned as he recalled Antje Molenaer's words in the kitchen. By Mrs. Molenaer's yardstick he could trust these men all right. If relishing food was the test, there wasn't a mean bone in any of them.

Suddenly he realized Mr. Barckaloe was beckoning to him and started forward.

"Mr. Ten Eyck's party is lighting pipes, Tinker," he said. "You'd better clear away their dishes and see that they have everything they want."

The boy's heart hammered. He hoped he wasn't so excited that he'd drop dishes like a clumsy oaf. Mr. Ten Eyck glanced up absently as Dirck began clearing plates. Then recognizing the boy, he smiled in friendly fashion.

"Why, it's Tinker Van Arsdalen. How come you're here, lad? I'd planned to stop by the lock tomorrow to thank you for getting the team and the carriage down here to the stable. The carriage maker says you did an ingenious patching job on that axle."

Turning to the men beside him at the table, Mr. Ten Eyck continued. "This boy jumped for my horses yesterday morning when we had an accident at the wharf. I have reason to be grateful, for he saved Tim a bad trampling and patched up the carriage besides.

"I think you must know Mr. Neilson, Tinker. This other gentleman is Mr. Guy Sylvester, the engineer in charge of the new lock repairs.

"Guy, young Tinker here is the son of the lockkeeper, Jacobus Van Arsdalen. You'll see him often, I expect, for he helps his father mornings down at the outlet. Now it seems he is working for Barckaloe the rest of the day. Am I right, Tinker?"

"Yes, sir. Mr. Barckaloe hired me yesterday when I brought your carriage down. That was a lucky errand you sent me on, Mr. Ten Eyck. The boy he had ran off and he was shorthanded. Is Tim all right now, sir? He looked rather shaky when you took him away."

"He's sore and bruised, Tinker, but he didn't break any bones. He says he wants to thank you himself. I've promised to bring him down to the lock."

Dirck flushed. "I'm glad he's all right, sir, but he hasn't anything to thank me for. I just happened to be standing close enough to grab the bays. That's really all, Mr. Ten Eyck." And Dirck carried his tray of dishes off to the kitchen.

Noticing Guy Sylvester's eyes follow him with approval, Mr. Ten Eyck spoke up. "He's worth watching, Guy, I think. You'll do me a favor if you keep an eye on him down at the lock. I suspect he's made for better things than tinkering."

"I agree with you, Nicholas. He looks promising. Keeping an eye on him may be doing the firm of Sylvester and Simcoe more of a favor than you." He glanced at his watch. "We mustn't stay too late, gentlemen. We have an engagement with Mr. Corlear, I think. James, can you see that clock on the wall behind me? This timepiece of mine seems to be running slow."

Lazily Mr. Neilson turned his head. "Better stick to your own, Guy," he advised. "Barckaloe's clock isn't even running slow; it's given up the ghost entirely."

The innkeeper, hearing the sound of his name, came over inquiringly.

"We need our bill, Staats, and you need your clock attended to," Ten Eyck told him. "Your guests will be missing their boats some morning." Then, catching sight of Dirck behind the trestle, he waved a hand in his direction. "Better put young Tinker to work on it. The smith claims he can mend anything."

Staats Barckaloe smiled broadly. "I had it in mind when I hired him, Mr. Ten Eyck. A tinker is a mighty handy man around an inn."

"There you are, Tinker," Mr. Ten Eyck laughed. "We've found another chore for you. Mind, we'll expect to see that clock running next time we all come to the Queen for supper."

Dirck looked at the innkeeper questioningly, and Mr. Barckaloe nodded. "I meant it," he said. "I'll see you have time to work on it soon. I kind of miss that clock myself."

CHAPTER FIVE

On the Banks

DIRCK RECONNOITERED the Brandt garden carefully on his way to the cornpatch next morning, but Maddy was not in sight. He felt distinctly aggrieved. She tagged at his heels for years, but when he really wanted her, she wasn't even visible. How was he going to tell her about Mr. Sylvester if she wasn't around? Any other day she'd be out by this time scrubbing the front steps.

He pulled weeds half heartedly, keeping one ear tuned for the sound of her footsteps, but he was on his way back to breakfast before he sighted Maddy waiting on his doorstep like an expectant puppy. Giving her an earsplitting whistle, he practically galloped the rest of the way.

Maddy danced impatiently. "I knew something exciting would happen. I had to set the bread or I'd have come before. Do hurry up and tell me, Dirck Van Arsdalen. Don't poke along like a turtle; talk just as fast as you can!"

Dirck grinned at her happily. The day was back to rights again.

"Maybe I will if you give me a chance," he retorted. "How am I going to tell you anything when you're blowing off like a safety valve?"

Hearing their voices, Mrs. Van Arsdalen appeared in the doorway.

"Bring Maddy in with you, Dirck," she said. "You can tell her all about last night while you eat your breakfast. Your father has to go to the deep lock with the engineers this morning, remember, and he'll expect you to take over at the outlet soon."

She watched the boy and girl talking earnestly at the table by the window.

I know Maddy spoils him, she admitted to herself, but she's good for him, too. Not like that empty-headed Schuyler girl he skated with this winter. He'll never get discouraged with Maddy around. I hope he never disappoints her; facing his failure would be harder for her than it would be for Dirck himself. Studying Maddy's intent, eager little face and Dirck's determined boyish chin, she felt reassured. Hard knocks won't hurt either of them permanently. They're built to weather any kind of storm.

Quick steps on the path outside made the three in the kitchen look up inquiringly just as a stocky, broad-shouldered young man turned in at the door.

"Why, Pieter!" exclaimed Mrs. Van Arsdalen joyously. "We didn't expect you till Sunday. It's good to see you, and you're just in time for breakfast."

Hastily she laid a place at the table and set out food for her older son. Pieter gave her a cheerful hug and hailed the two at the table good-naturedly. "Morning, young ones. You look as though you were plotting something with your heads together like that. Maddy, aren't you afraid Dirck will turn you into a tinker, too, one of these days?"

Maddy didn't even have to think that over. "Why, Pieter, I wouldn't mind a bit. Then Dirck and I could travel all over like gypsies. We'll stop at your parsonage and mend all your pots and pans," she promised.

"I'll remember that," Pieter assured her, "and right now I'm nearer to a parsonage than I've ever been. That's why I'm home, Mother. The seminary is sending me to Staten Island today for six weeks to fill a pulpit where the pastor's sick. It'll be wonderful experience, of course, and anyway I didn't have any choice in the matter. I just hope the people aren't too critical."

Detecting a faintly anxious note in Pieter's voice, Dirck smiled at his brother confidently. "You'll be successful, Pieter, never fear. Maybe you'll be scared at first, but the congregation will never guess it. You'll look like a regular pastor right off!"

Mrs. Van Arsdalen nodded agreement. "Dirck's right, Pieter. You'll do well, I know. Your father is going to be very pleased about this, son. Go along down to the outlet with Dirck and tell him about it while I lay out fresh clothes for your journey. You can stop by for them before you go back to school."

From the window, she watched the two boys stride down the path together. How different they were: Dirck, lean and rangy, his dark head topping his heavier set, blond brother by a good four inches.

She sighed. "At least Pieter's feet are set firmly on his chosen path, Maddy. I wish I could see ahead for Dirck, too."

"Dirck will be an engineer, Mrs. Van Arsdalen." The

girl's voice was calmly assured. "You'll be as proud of his canals and bridges as you'll be of Pieter in his pulpit." Laughter and excitement bubbled back into her voice. "They'll both be famous for you, I know they will— only, of course, Dirck will be even more famous than Pieter."

Her emphatic loyalty set Mrs. Van Arsdalen's eyes dancing. "I expect you're right, Maddy. He'll be an engineer somehow, a famous one of course. Dirck's a little like the tow mules, you know: stubborn when he takes a notion."

But Maddy refused to be baited. "That's a sign he's so Dutch he can't be beaten," she declared triumphantly and skipped out the door for home.

Down at the outlet the boys found their father ready for Dirck to take over. Pieter's visit surprised him, but his pleasure at his son's news was hearty. Clearly, to Jacobus Van Arsdalen his older son's choice of a profession was a matter of increasing pride, and he looked eagerly forward to the day when he should see Pieter ordained and perhaps hear him preach in their own Dutch Church in New Brunswick. Now, thinking of the trip to Staten Island, he cast a weatherwise eye at the sky.

"No rain in sight yet, boys. Pieter will have a pleasant journey downriver. Anyway he'll be cooler than you'll be, Dirck, down at the Queen." He eyed his younger son quizzically. "I expect this lad's told you all about his new work, Pieter. He's finding it much to his liking so far."

"Of course he likes it, Father. There's always something interesting at the Queen. You won't even need the *Guard-*

ian and *Advertiser* any more; Dirck will have all the news."
Pieter gave his brother an affectionate slap on the back by
way of good-by. "Coming along to the house to meet your
engineer, Father? Your substitute here looks ready to take
over, and I'm going back that way to pick up my clothes
and say good-by to Mother."

Mr. Van Arsdalen nodded. It was time he was off. "Call
on Johann Brandt if you need help any time, Dirck. He's
home this morning. I expect I'll be back when the sun's
high."

Dirck's eyes followed them with pride. How fine looking
they are, he thought, and almost exactly alike. If Pieter
just had Father's height, you'd really think they were
twins!

The morning passed swiftly for Dirck, kept busy with
the long strings of tows going out the canal toward New
York. Bargemen tossed him bits of news and banter as they
manipulated their boats through the locks. Free of the tow
mules now, they bent their backs to their poles and floated
out into the river to be picked up by waiting tugs and
hauled along again, as many as a hundred in a single tow.
They were a lusty, brawling lot, these rafters, big and
brawny and noisy. Dirck couldn't imagine the river without them. Their horseplay, their laughter, their sudden
quarrels were warp and woof of his memories.

Toward midmorning when there was a lull in the tangle
of barges moving downstream, Dirck strolled out on the
turntable catwalk over the gates for a casual check. Everything was in order, except for a plank half sprung in the
upper level of the gate. Back he went for nails and ham-

mer; then, astride the gate, dangling his bare feet contentedly in the water, he set to work.

Nails were something you took for granted, he mused;
nobody paid them much heed, but patching must have
been a regular chore when things had to be pegged together. That well stairway at the Queen, for instance,
curving in a beautiful spiral to the top floor and not a
nail in it—that baffled him. Try as he would, he had never
figured out how it had been put together.

Satisfied that the plank was fast, Dirck prepared to
scramble back to the bank. He had banged away so noisily
he hadn't realized anyone was around, yet here was his
father in the middle of a swarm of men. And one of the
men was Mr. Sylvester. Apparently the engineer had finished inspecting the deep lock early enough to take a look
at the outlet, too, before dinner. Hastily pocketing his
hammer, Dirck jumped down to the ground and made his
way to his father's side.

"My son Dirck, gentlemen," Mr. Van Arsdalen presented him to the group. "He's been my substitute this
forenoon; a bit on the light side if it comes to crew trouble
perhaps, but we don't have much hereabouts any more."

A couple of the men looked at the big lockkeeper and
laughed. "You have a reputation, Van Arsdalen. Even the
Hoboken crews mind their manners when you're on the
bank, we hear. A broken head is a great teacher."

Jacobus chuckled drily and led the way to the lockside.
Dirck tagged contentedly along. Since his father hadn't
dismissed him, he felt free to follow and watch. He eyed
the visitors at the lock with interest. Most of them, he

knew, were directors of the canal company. Mr. Sylvester seemed to be the only representative of his engineering firm on hand at the moment. It was going to be wonderful to hang around when the work really got under way. He could hardly wait. Standing at the edge of the group, Dirck watched Mr. Sylvester mount the catwalk and peer down at the gates below, then turn and ask a question of the lockkeeper close beside him. Jacobus promptly walked back to the bank.

"Mr. Sylvester thinks he can use you, son," he called. "Go on up and get his instructions."

Dirck needed no prodding. He was heading for the engineer almost before his father finished speaking. "Father says you want me, sir."

Mr. Sylvester nodded. "You seem the likeliest prospect, Tinker." He glanced at the men on the bank and chuckled. "Somehow I can't quite fancy any of those gentlemen astride the gates down below. Think you can manage a few measurements for me?"

"Of course, sir."

"Good. Here, put this rule in your pocket and climb down. Call the figures up to me as I ask for them and give me time to jot them down. We'll recheck if we need to."

Tucking the rule securely away, Dirck climbed over the handrails and dropped down on the slippery gates. Then, once more balanced astride, he signed that he was ready. Mr. Sylvester's orders were crisp and clear, and sliding along, the unfolded rule in his hand, Dirck called careful measurements as they were wanted. Twice the engineer, leaning over the rail above the boy, asked for another check before he was satisfied, but the task was not a long one. Dirck was surprised when Mr. Sylvester announced that he was through.

"That'll do, Tinker, I think," he called. "Remarkable, really, how well these figures tally with the old ones in spite of wear and tear and natural warping. The repair work won't be as bad as the company expects—and I guess that won't hurt their feelings any either, with the project for deepening and widening the canal already emptying their purses. Thank you, Tinker, for lending a hand."

"I liked doing it, Mr. Sylvester," Dirck said, as he climbed back on the catwalk. "Any kind of job around the locks suits me. And now if you'll excuse me, sir, I'd better see if Father wants anything before I have to get ready to go to the Queen."

He strode away, and Guy Sylvester sought out his associates who had drifted over to the shade of a clump of willows.

"Well, gentlemen, I've had a quick look. Unless we find something unexpected when we start work, your refitting job still looks routine and will work right into the enlarging process. Suppose we go in search of dinner and talk the matter over as we dine."

The idea of food was visibly bracing, and taking prompt leave of the two Van Arsdalens, the visitors made straight for their carriages strung out along Burnet Street wherever the coachmen could find a patch of shelter from the sun. Jacobus knocked out his pipe.

"They set us a good example, eh, Dirck? With this heat

47

a lookout from the window will be enough for at least an hour at noontime, or our bargemen aren't as much like yonder gentlemen as I think."

Side by side, father and son entered the kitchen door, glad to relax for a time and quite positive that the stove couldn't be half so hot as the sun that had been broiling them all morning. To Dirck, breakfast had begun to seem like something out of past history over an hour ago, and the smell of baked shad, fresh from the Raritan, set his mouth watering. He ate in happy silence. It puzzled him sometimes how women could do all that talking at table and still get anything to eat. He fetched a sigh of contentment. It began to look as though he might last till supper after all.

"I expect I'd better be off, Mother. I'll bring you a couple of pails of water first." Halfway out the door, he paused. "I nearly forgot the cooling pail. Shall I stow anything away besides the butter?"

"A jug of cider, please, son. With the weather what it is, your father will be glad of it later on. And, mind, Dirck, lower the pail way down in the well. It's too hot to leave food right on the surface."

Ten minutes later the boy was waving good-by. "Jug's in the cooling pail, Mother, and the water bucket's on the bench. I'll be home as soon as Mr. Barckaloe is finished with me. Don't wait up if I'm late."

CHAPTER SIX

The Ibis and the Alligator

IT WAS MUCH too hot to hurry. Dirck unconsciously slowed his pace, clinging to the shadow of buildings whenever he could and thinking longingly of the swimming hole in the boxes by the deep lock. Half the boys in town would be diving in before the afternoon ended. He began to plot playing hooky from the Queen for just about an hour later on. The only trouble was Antje Molenaer; with her around he knew he'd never get away with it. Her sharp eye made the schoolmaster seem half-blind in comparison. Thinking of Mrs. Molenaer quickened his step, and he swung across the foot of Hiram Street at a good clip.

Ahead of him, down by the Sturdevandt shipyards, something seemed to be going on. A lot of people were turning in; he could hear them chattering and laughing way up the block. As he drew nearer, he began to recognize some of them. Mr. Neilson climbed out of his carriage and joined the other canal directors who had visited the locks with Mr. Sylvester that morning. Across the way, Maddy's father left his harness shop and strolled over to the throng jamming the gate. Mr. Fitten, the town marshall, and some of the city-watch hurried in from Albany Street and began to scatter among the crowd. Dirck knew they were on the lookout for pickpockets and trouble-makers.

Full of curiosity, he shinnied up the nearest tree and peered over people's heads toward the waterfront. The queerest looking contraption he'd ever seen afloat was tied up in the canal; it looked more like a huge wooden slice of pie than a boat. Hastily he jumped down and looked around for a chance to squirm through the crowd. If he could squeeze in somewhere, he could get a glimpse of that thing nearer at hand and then walk along the canal bank to Albany Street without being late enough to get in trouble at the Queen.

Darting around the fringes of the throng, he trotted toward a couple of broken palings he remembered spotting the other day on the far side of the fence. One thing he didn't want, though, was a flock of small boys tagging at his heels when he wriggled out on the other side; that'd be a sure way to get himself chased out before he saw any-thing. Looking hurriedly back over his shoulder to be sure he wasn't tagged, Dirck rounded the fence corner and bumped hard into someone substantial enough to knock the wind nearly out of him. Gasping, he looked quickly round to find Staats Barckaloe facing him.

"Rushing to work, young Tinker, or to the break in the fence yonder?" he drawled.

Dirck looked a bit shamefaced, caught like a small boy playing a trick. He watched his employer uncertainly for a minute until the twinkle in the innkeeper's eye reassured him.

"It's a nice-sized break, Mr. Barckaloe," he suggested. "We can both make it by squeezing a mite. There's a queer sort of float down the canal worth looking at. Shall we try it?"

His voice was so persuasive that the innkeeper chuckled.

"We'll steal a march on the rest of them filing through the gate, Tinker. Go ahead and pry those palings apart. If I stick in the middle, you can jimmy me out."

Puffing and grunting, the innkeeper worked his bulk part way through the fence.

"Here, give me a pull, young fellow, or I'm stuck till Doomsday. A fine fix for a respectable tavern keeper to get caught in. Look lively, lad, I think I hear somebody coming!"

There was such genuine alarm in his voice that Dirck reached out hastily and yanked him through the gap before he lost his dignity altogether. Red-faced and rumpled, he began to set himself to rights, grumbling good-naturedly that the boy slipped through like an eel.

"It's Antje's cooking does it; had a waistline myself before she took over the kitchen. Now where's this contraption you're so curious about? I thought this was just a routine launching today."

Together they walked across the busy yards. Staats Barckaloe's presence was taken for granted, and Dirck sailed along contentedly in his wake.

"There it is, Mr. Barckaloe," Dirck pointed. "Did you ever see a barge like that before?"

The innkeeper craned his neck. "Bless my soul," he muttered, "it's the old packet John Stevens built twenty years ago when we thought we'd have regular passenger service on the canal. I wonder where they dug that up?"

Pleased as a child, Staats hurried Dirck forward, reminiscing happily. "That barge was built over in Hoboken," he told the boy, "and you've never seen anything else like it because it's the only one that ever did get built. Lord, but we were proud when we first set eyes on her. She belonged to the Delaware and Raritan Packet Line, and when she was built they just ignored the four-mile-an-hour speed limit fixed for the freight barges. With sixty passengers piled on board, she pulled along at a steady ten-mile-an-hour clip. Running time between New Brunswick and Philadelphia only nine and a half hours! What a boat!

"But the packet line petered out," he said sadly; "couldn't compete with the railroads, Tinker, too slow. We Americans are always in such a tarnation hurry." He shook his head disgustedly. "It's a national weakness, bound to ruin our digestion and set us by the ears. Public men with the colic can't think straight; their minds are fixed on their stomachs."

Dirck gave polite ear-service to the innkeeper's strictures on his countrymen's habits, but his interest centered on the packet boat. Fascinated, he studied her queer lines.

"She must be a hundred feet long, Mr. Barckaloe," he exclaimed, "and narrow! Why, she's no more than eight feet wide anywhere. And look at her prow, sir; it's sharp as a wedge. No wonder she pulled easy. She can't draw more than fifteen inches."

"You should have seen her in service, Tinker." Staats' tone was as fond as if he'd designed the barge himself.

"Old Tise Sollom captained her as long as she ran; called the *Ibis* she was, for some foreign bird or other. She carried an awning and sixty armchairs all cushioned in plum color. And her horses curried within an inch of their lives! No mules for the *Ibis;* she was too proud."

He gestured with his head in the direction of the big crowd farther along the bank. "Yet with all her folderols, she didn't cost as much as those two coal barges over there that Sturdevandt is launching in a minute. Thirty-two dollars a ton for that new *Shark* and that *Alligator,* he tells me, what with labor and materials ballooning right up. Still, I guess the cost won't frighten the shareholders any; not with transportation tonnage running over the two-million mark, it won't, my lad."

Just then the talk and laughter died away. Mounted on the ribs of a half-finished barge, Looe Sturdevandt was beginning a speech of welcome. Off at the edge of the group, Dirck could catch only snatches of what he was saying.

"Ladies and gentlemen—a happy occasion—the past and the future of our great canal united—the hope of the Sturdevandt shipyards that these new barges give long and honest service. Now we invite you all to board the old-fashioned *Ibis* and the newest barge our progressive age has designed."

Amid thunderous applause, he signaled to the workmen. Winches creaked; cables, released from stays, rattled over pulleys; foremen shouted instructions. A resounding splash, closely followed by a second, and the *Shark* and the *Alligator* were afloat.

Dirck looked at Mr. Barckaloe inquiringly, but that gentleman shook his head.

"I'll hang about a bit and look the floats over. Tell Antje I'll be along shortly. Custom will be brisk when this is over or I miss my guess."

Brisk was hardly the word for it, Dirck thought as he dashed back and forth between kitchen and common room an hour later; overwhelming was more like it. His eyes smarted from the fog of pipe smoke, and his ears buzzed from the din of voices. The sight of the *Ibis* had opened a floodgate of memories, and the older men were seining up stories faster than the shadders on the river ever hauled up their fish.

Over in one corner a group of young fellows was greeting a late arrival and chafing him good-humoredly for missing the ceremonies at Sturdevandt's.

"Late as usual. Gad, Court, and you don't mend your ways, you'll be late for your wedding. We don't envy Gerardus his job as groomsman."

Court Van Voorhees settled himself comfortably. "I'll still be alive, my bucks, when you've all raced yourselves into early graves. But never worry; I'll keep them green for you and shed an occasional tear."

He smiled at them cheerfully, dodging a tobacco pouch tossed at his head.

"What'll you have, gentlemen? I'm going to need refreshment if you're planning to bring me up to date in the best *Guardian and Advertiser* style. Just don't make your tale too stimulating; remember I was toiling when you butterflies were fluttering around the canal banks."

Spying Dirck hovering nearby, he beckoned the boy over for orders.

"Hello, Tinker," he said. "Mr. Ten Eyck told me you were around. It'll be a pleasant change to have someone who isn't glued to the floor; you could grow a whole crop of hay under the feet of that last boy. Next time Staats Barckaloe passes this way I'll be glad to give him a first-hand account of your speed, especially in apple orchards. Anything to oblige an old friend."

Dirck grinned. "I guess I'd get along better without that recommendation. You had too sharp an eye, Mr. Court; none of us ever got away with anything from the Van Voorhees trees. We always used to say it was because you'd been so good at filching apples yourself."

"Got you there, Court," Gerardus De Peyster laughed. "He'd never dare split on you, Tinker; his own past won't stand it."

"My brother Pieter went to school with him awhile, Mr. Gerry. I've heard so many stories that I guess I'm safe— anyway till I get back with your orders."

Filling their mugs at the big keg in the scullery, Dirck began wondering if the banter he'd overheard had meant anything, whether Court Van Voorhees was really going to get married. He supposed he'd choose some girl from New York. He had even gone to school there for a couple of years, living with his mother's people somewhere. It'd be a pity if the girl didn't like a small town and persuaded him off to New York.

He found an answer sooner than he expected. Waiting on Mr. Neilson and Mr. Corlear shortly, he saw Mr. Cor-

56

lear nod toward the group of young men in the corner.

"There's Ten Eyck's prospective son-in-law, James, young Courtland Van Voorhees. He's marrying Ann Augusta in September. A good lad from a good family. I'm glad he's settling down here where his family roots are deep."

Mr. Neilson smiled. "So is Nicholas. He keeps his daughter nearby and acquires a son he's proud to have. He was afraid for a while that she'd pick young Gerritse and move to Albany. I met him this morning down at the steamboat, off to order a ruby necklace as a wedding present for his girl. He was pleased as punch and prepared to order the moon if she hinted she wanted it. Can't say I blame him either. Ann Augusta's as fine as girls come and pretty enough to turn any man's head." He looked over at Court Van Voorhees again. "It couldn't be a better match."

Privately Dirck thought so, too. Like every other younger boy in town, he had made a hero of big, laughing Court Van Voorhees, who did everything better than anyone else, and the habit still persisted. A girl as pretty as Ann Augusta Ten Eyck was exactly what he deserved. And turning down this Gerritse, whoever he was, to choose Court showed she had a lot more sense than most girls.

He fell to dreaming. Probably someday Pieter would get married, too, not to anybody like Ann Augusta, of course, but maybe to some girl who came to his church and fell in love with the pastor.

Naturally he'd never get married himself. An engineer didn't really settle down to living in a house, and a girl was likely to be all baked into shape before a fellow could train her to live in shacks and tents. Chances were nowadays if a girl met up with a bear or fell in a river, she'd get killed, and an engineer couldn't decently risk his wife like that. Anyway, he knew he'd be too busy to bother with girls.

Probably it would be a good idea to persuade Maddy to teach him about cooking. When they went fishing, she managed to get a regular meal right over a campfire on the towpath. If he could do that, he wouldn't starve even if he had a bad camp cook like the one that Mr. Sylvester told about last night. Absent-mindedly picturing himself at work on magnificent bridges over jungle rivers, Dirck stood square in the center of the room, a tray of dishes clutched in his arms, until Mrs. Molenaer, thoroughly indignant, sent Katje in from the kitchen to prod him out of his dreams.

CHAPTER SEVEN

Shoring

DIRCK STUDIED every step of the canal-widening with absorption. The outlet gates stood wide open most of the time. Swarms of workmen, hefty Irishmen from New York, added the rattle of shovels and the clank of dredges to the shouts of wagoners hauling supplies. Before their attacks, the bank at the lower end of the canal gradually began to move back. It was slow, laborious work, cutting, digging, and dredging. Whole wagonloads of rock and timber lined the shore. Down in the water, men in high boots pounded stone into the raw earth of each new section of bank and manipulated eight-by-eights over the edge to drive in shoring posts and spike heavy planks against them.

A flagman posted just below the Toll Bridge at Albany Street signaled relays of watchmen down the towpath when barges were floated into the boxes back of the deep lock. In turn, they flagged the warning on to Jacobus at the outlet. At a blast of his horn workmen scrambled hastily out of the low water, the lock gates closed, and signals wigwagged their way back up the towpath. Not long afterward, the deep lock open, water raced heavily

59

along the canal bed, and nimble-footed tow mules hove into sight, their drivers urging them on in voices that would have done credit to a foghorn. Behind them, the barges towed slowly, piled high with coal. As they moved sluggishly downstream, their crews opened with volleys of scathing comment for the benefit of the workmen on shore, and to a man, the Irish answered back, roaring insults until the last bargeman had floated through the reopened gates into the river.

Once more the water was back at a workable level, auxiliary pumps wheezed into motion, men swung down over the bank, and sledge hammers fell on wooden posts with the sharp, challenging rhythm of a primitive log drum. A half-hour later the whole process might have to be repeated again. The cycle was endless.

The work at the lock itself, though, interested Dirck most. Doggedly studying the blueprints tacked up on the winch shack, he figured out the general plan. The widening of the canal began to taper off some yards above the outlet, and as nearly as Dirck could judge, the plans called for adding just a couple of feet more space to the feed-in and outlet combined. But how Mr. Sylvester was going to add even those feet without losing enough water to tie up traffic completely was what puzzled him.

Spending every minute he could at the locks, Dirck watched eagerly to see what would happen. Small crews of picked men worked steadily on the construction of new gates, wider and heavier than the old. Piece by piece, planks were reenforced and bolt after bolt made tight. Lying on the bank just below the outlet, both new gates slowly grew solid enough to be hoisted into place when the time came. Meanwhile, six-foot cedar logs, sharpened to stakes at the bottom, began to bristle on the bank. Set close like the logs of a frontier palisade, they ran out in a line from the old gate about two feet and then at a right angle along the shore toward town.

Watching intently one morning, Dirck realized how exactly they were set to come in precisely in line with the completed section of the new bank. Mr. Sylvester, noticing the boy's eager interest, stopped for a word.

"Look mighty like a stockade fence, don't they, Tinker? Once they're driven deep, though, they'll be an effective breakwater, and we'll slice away that bank without losing water enough to tie up the outlet while we work. We'll have to haul out that row by the lock when we swing the new gates, of course, but along the side here they'll stay right in for shoring. You learn to kill two birds with one stone in this business; it saves time and tempers."

The sound of Jacobus's horn made them both turn to glance upstream. Workmen were climbing back on the bank, snatching gladly at a moment to wipe their steaming faces and down a mug of water from buckets on the shore. Then in the wake of the water refilling the canal, a barge floated gradually into sight, her crew blurred figures in the distance. Closer and closer she came to the noisy accompaniment of jeers from the workmen.

"Sure and it's an aisy loife, lyin' around all day on the soft coal. Look at thim, Tim, how tender and gentle they be; 'tis the loafin' does it."

Dirck chuckled. The Irishman's sketch of gentle, easygoing rafters delighted him. He watched the approaching barge, ready to wave a greeting to any old friends in the crew.

"Why, it's one of the new barges, Mr. Sylvester—the big one they call the *Alligator*. Verne Giles captains her, Father says, but his crew's strange, picked up downriver most likely. She can do with those feet you're adding, can't she, sir? It would be close hauling to pass beside her the way the canal's been."

Mr. Sylvester nodded. "Right you are, Tinker. She was built with the new proportions in mind."

They watched while the rafters rid the *Alligator* of her towlines and made ready to float out into the river. Dirck found himself listening automatically with her crew for the creaking of the winches that would signal the outlet gate was opening up. Suddenly he realized something was wrong and started for the shack.

"Winch is stuck, I guess, sir," he called back over his shoulder. "Father may need a hand."

The engineer on his heels, the boy ran up to the shack where Jacobus was working on the machinery, a length of loosened cable tangled in the cogs. Dropping to his knees, Dirck began to help, following his father's orders carefully. Bit by bit, they worked the cable free and slipped it back in place. The machinery lumbered into action as Jacobus cranked, and the Van Arsdalens got contentedly to their feet. Someday the winch might win one of their occasional tussles and refuse to budge; this time they were victors again.

Guy Sylvester had watched Jacobus's confident hands with approval. Now he spoke up.

"You'd have made an engineer, Van Arsdalen. Didn't you ever give the idea a thought?"

"Who me?" Jacobus Van Arsdalen looked so dumbfounded that his son had to turn his head away to hide a grin. "Can't say I did, though I thought some of blacksmithing it for a spell. We're plain people, mostly carpenters; engineering isn't in our line."

The engineer eyed him shrewdly for a moment before he answered.

"Plain people aplenty in my business, Van Arsdalen. Anyway, young Tinker here comes by the skill in his hands honestly."

And nodding to them both, he strode out the door.

Dirck wanted to cheer. "Plain people aplenty in my business!" Mr. Sylvester was an ally worth having, even if he didn't realize he was one. He stole a glance at his father, but Jacobus was absently stuffing his pipe, a slight frown on his forehead. The boy started to speak and thought better of it. Quietly he slipped out and back to the locks, where Maddy found him when she ran across the fields a few minutes later.

Nearly bursting at the seams with excitement, Dirck recounted the episode in the winch shack.

"You should have seen Father's face, Maddy; you should have seen how queer he looked!"

The girl's eyes danced. "Mr. Sylvester will be on your side, Dirck. I know he will."

Gathering her skirts carefully, she swept him a formal curtsy.

"Mr. Van Arsdalen, the famous engineer, I believe."

Dirck laughed happily. Maddy's certainty was contagious. Sure of his audience's interest, he led her along the bank to see the shoring and back again to the lock so he could explain about the cedar logs. Full of curiosity, the girl balanced casually on the slippery moss of the bank just beyond the outlet and leaned over to watch the crews at work. Suddenly a firm hand grasped her shoulder and pulled her back.

Mr. Sylvester's voice was reproving. "You may have a good hand for tools, Tinker, but you've none for the lady's safety."

Taken aback, Dirck gulped a couple of times before he got his words out. "But this is Maddy Brandt, sir!"

Mr. Sylvester bowed. "I'm delighted to meet Miss Maddy, Tinker, but I confess I don't follow your reasoning. That bank's slippery. Any girl can fall into deep water, can't she?"

Maddy smiled at the tall engineer. "Oh, Dirck just means I'm used to that slippery bank, Mr. Sylvester."

"And she's a regular water rat, sir," the boy chimed in. "A ducking wouldn't hurt her a bit."

"Father taught me to swim, sir," Maddy explained. "Mother was always afraid I'd drown playing on the river with Dirck, so Father fixed it so she wouldn't worry any. I can manage my skirts all right in the water. You needn't worry a bit, Mr. Sylvester, even if I fall in."

Guy Sylvester chuckled. "So you teach your girls to swim here. I learn something new about New Brunswickers every day. Still," his voice was dry, "I'd prefer you right side up on the bank, young lady. See that you keep an eye on her, Tinker. My workmen don't know your New Brunswick ways, and one of them might drown jumping in to rescue her."

Maddy and Dirck looked startled. "We never thought of that, Mr. Sylvester," the boy exclaimed. "Maddy will just have to be careful if she wants to stay around here. Maybe she ought to go home anyway. Girls don't belong around engineering jobs."

Maddy ignored him calmly and turned to the engineer. "I don't believe Mr. Sylvester minds a bit if I stay."

"Not a bit," he assured her cheerfully. "I'm used to womenfolk around our construction jobs: my partner's wife and mine both go along with us to all sorts of outlandish places. Better not let them hear you say 'girls don't belong around engineering jobs,' young Tinker. They thought New Brunswick would be too civilized for them, but they'll be coming down to visit one of these days."

Grinning at Dirck's discomfiture, the engineer headed up the shore, leaving Maddy annoyingly triumphant. The sound of the Van Arsdalen dinner horn jogged her memory.

"Oh, Dirck, I nearly forgot what I came for. If I bring Aunt Antje's eggs over right after dinner, Mother wondered if you'd take them to the Queen this once? She needs me to help with the preserving." Maddy's voice suddenly sounded as though it had been dipped in a jam pot.

Dirck grinned at her. "You can change your tune fast when you want something, Maddy Brandt, but I suppose I'll do it if your mother wants me to."

Maddy gave him a dazzling smile and hurried off. Reluctantly Dirck headed for the house himself. Where the mornings went, he didn't know. Nowadays it always seemed time to eat and rush off to the Queen. Still, he couldn't rear back on his haunches like a balky mule. He'd been working regularly five weeks now, and the little bag of money in his clothes press was perceptibly heavier. He hugged the thought of those dollars to him like a miser. Ten dollars he'd had to start with, saved bit by bit from all sorts of odd jobs. Now every time he added to them, they spelled Rutgers more distinctly. If he could get the whole twenty-three dollars for first term tuition, and if Mr. Barckaloe let him keep his job nights to take care of the next bill, maybe his father would give in, and he'd really be in college by September. Whenever he thought of that, he walked to the Queen with his head bumping against rainbows, almost forgetting how much he hated to miss all the activities at the locks.

Perhaps today he'd get a chance to tackle the clock again. Dirck took good care that the innkeeper had no cause for complaint; he wasn't taking any chances with a job like his, but working on the Connecticut clock was a lot more interesting than most of his chores at the Queen. The case was still on the wall, but he had the works spread out on a plank table in a little storeroom where no one would bother them. Clockwork had proved complicated. He'd had to make a diagram so every piece would get back in the right place when he'd cleaned and oiled them all up. It was slow work even when Mr. Barckaloe could spare him for a while, but at least he had it all figured out now and knew what he was doing.

Someday, he hoped, he could get his hands on a broken clock nobody wanted and fix it for his mother. He knew how much she wanted one. Just as much as I want to study mathematics at Rutgers, I guess, he thought to himself as he turned in the kitchen door.

CHAPTER EIGHT

Crew Trouble

MR. VAN ARSDALEN came in to dinner a bit late. "Almost didn't come at all, Margaretta," he said, "but my appetite got the better of me. Verne Giles tied the *Alligator* up down below the outlet, and I don't like the looks of that crew he's got. They're spoiling for trouble. I hoped he'd float on down and hitch onto his tug until the rest of the string come through. The *Shark's* tied up, too, worse luck, and it's too hot today to be settling German-Irish battles."

He wiped his face and smiled at his wife as she began serving.

"Maybe you're just borrowing trouble, Jacobus," she said comfortably. "And if you're not, you'll handle it a whole lot easier once you've had dinner. Not a mite of use getting all riled up until there's something to be riled about. Just forget about it now and tell me what I'd better do about Mr. Sylvester."

At Jacobus's puzzled look, she smiled. She'd taken his mind off his nuisancesome rafters for a bit.

"He stopped by this morning to see if I'd give him meals noondays. Seems it's hard to leave the job to go all the way back to the Queen right now. I said I'd talk to you and let him know later."

She paused expectantly, and Jacobus frowned in thought.

"Can't see any harm in it, Margaretta," he said slowly, "not if you don't mind extra work, weather like this."

"Just a few more dishes, Jacobus; no real work at all." Mrs. Van Arsdalen spoke briskly. "That's settled then. He wants to pay fifteen cents, same as he pays at the Queen, though I warned him he'd get no fancy food. I must say he didn't appear to worry any; just allowed you looked pretty well fed."

Jacobus laughed contentedly. "He'll find your cooking will do," he assured her. "No complaints of his camp cook on this job. Between you and Antje, he'll likely get fat as a Christmas goose." He eyed his son speculatively for a minute. "I guess this arrangement suits Dirck here fine. He's been finding Mr. Sylvester pretty interesting."

"I don't get in his way, Father," the boy protested. "I just like to watch, and sometimes he stops to explain things to me. He knows so much I'd like to know. And what do you think he told Maddy today—that his wife goes to all sorts of queer places with him!"

"Mercy on us," Mrs. Van Arsdalen exclaimed. "If Wilhelmina Brandt thinks he's putting any more roving notions in that child's head, she'll keep her under lock and key. She blames them all on Dirck now, but I don't know what she expects; I declare I don't. Maddy's the spittin' image of her Grandmother Brandt, and I've heard Johann yarn a dozen times about how she helped chop trees to build a cabin in the wilderness around Albany and shot goodness knows how many Indians with her own gun."

She stopped to draw an indignant breath.

Jacobus and Dirck roared with laughter at her ruffled feathers.

"Maybe I should have been an engineer the way Mr. Sylvester suggested this morning, Margaretta. Then you could have gone pioneering, too." Her husband's eyes twinkled at her horrified look.

"No thank you, Jacobus," she said firmly. "My grandmother didn't scalp Indians. She lived right comfortably beside the Zuider Zee. I like you just as you are: the New Brunswick lockkeeper with a house beside the canal. You can let Dirck go out and do any engineering in this family."

Dirck's heart swelled. His mother hadn't let her opportunity slip. But Jacobus didn't answer. His head was cocked toward the open kitchen window.

"Was that a yowl?" His voice was sharp.

"Regular Comanche war whoop, Father." Dirck jumped to his feet.

"I knew it," the lockkeeper muttered. "Those rafters have busted loose." He was out the door in two strides. "Coming, son?" he called back, and Dirck pelted headlong after him down the path to the lock.

On the shore below the outlet bedlam had broken out. A roaring circle of Irishmen was bellowing encouragement to its champions struggling furiously with the crews of the two barges. Holy St. Patrick! Insult the Irish, would they! Stamping their feet, they howled frantic approval whenever a blow landed on a bargeman's head. Jacobus's angry shout was swallowed up unnoticed in the general fury. Knocking men about like ninepins, he pushed his way through the ring of spectators and plunged into the fighting mass. Dirck was only a second behind him.

No need to tell either Van Arsdalen what had happened. They knew the story of old. Bored by inactivity, the rafters had amused themselves taunting the workmen, and a couple of hotheads had struck sparks. This fight was bigger than usual, that's all. Between the crews and the Irish, fully thirty men were involved.

Tugging away to break clinches, Dirck punched methodically whenever he saw a chance. A brawny fist landed high on his cheekbone, snapping his head back and making him dizzy. Grimly he shook his head to clear it and swung heavily at a bargeman whooping down on him. Jacobus suddenly materialized at his side to grab two mouthing fighters and knock their heads together. Then he dropped out of sight again, lost somewhere in the see-saw struggle.

Back from dinner at the Queen, Guy Sylvester sent excited small boys scurrying upshore for a half-dozen foremen. Wading into the yelling onlookers himself, he systematically yanked man after man out of the ranks. One look at his face settled most of them; a hard fist quelled the rebels. It was one thing to howl yourself hoarse watching a fight, quite another to lose a job defying the boss. Foremen coming on the run plunged through the disintegrating mob into the fight. Rid of the onlookers who had cluttered his view, Mr. Sylvester stopped to take stock. He caught a momentary glimpse of Jacobus. The huge lock-keeper was bruised and panting, but he gave no sign of real distress. Apparently he had already spotted the re-enforcements the engineer had sent him and was sure of a quick finish. Dirck was harder to sight. He was still giving a good account of himself, Guy Sylvester finally discovered, but he'd taken a fearful mauling. His face was bleeding badly, and one eye had swelled nearly shut.

Watching his chance, the engineer sent one bargeman sprawling and knocked a charging Irishman head over heels. With grim satisfaction, he noted that they stayed where they fell. An uppercut to the jaw promptly sent another man to join them. Balanced on his toes, he waited patiently for an opening and a chance to pounce.

Maddy, flying across the meadow, her basket of eggs swinging precariously on her arm, saw Mr. Sylvester first. His cool precision as he swung a hard blow was reassuring. Quickly her eyes darted over the fighters, trying to find the Van Arsdalens. Dirck's tired, swollen face sent an angry tingle along her spine. If she were only a boy, she'd jump in there and batter anyone who came near him.

Furious at her own helplessness, she watched every maneuver. Only about a dozen bargemen and laborers were still on their feet, and most of them were weaving unsteadily. Maddy began to feel better; it must be almost over now.

Then suddenly she cried out in terror. A frenzied bargeman had caught up half a broken oar and was swinging it over Dirck's head. Unable to warn him above the din, she tried frantically to think of something, anything she could throw. The basket on her arm caught her eye. Quickly her hand darted in and swung back, clutching an egg. Her lips set hard, she threw straight from the shoulder, concentrating on the speed and accuracy Dirck had drilled into her with a ball. She was almost crying now; she'd aimed too high; she knew she had.

Then the egg landed. Square between the bargeman's eyes it smashed to pieces, spilling its sticky contents down his face. Bewildered, the man let his arm waver for a moment. But the oar struck—a sharp, glancing blow along the back of Dirck's head. The boy swayed, struggling wildly to recover his balance before he slumped forward to the ground. In despair Maddy buried her face in her arm, her shoulders shaking. A cool touch on her hand and an admiring voice steadied her.

"Quick thinking, Miss Maddy. Your wits saved Tinker a fractured skull."

She looked up at Mr. Sylvester wonderingly. "You mean he's not badly hurt? But he fell, sir. The oar landed; I saw it myself!"

The engineer smiled. "Not hard enough to mean more than a goose egg I hope. But come along, and we'll see for ourselves."

Dirck's unconscious figure had been carried down to the canal bank, and Court Van Voorhees, who had happened along toward the end of the fight, was on his knees in the grass scooping handfuls of water over the boy's cut and swollen face. Sputtering a bit, Dirck groggily opened his good eye and struggled upright.

"Here, none of that! You'll land me in the guardhouse."

Court gently forced the boy back. "Your mother left strict orders to keep you flat while she fetched salve, and she had fire in her eye, Tinker. I'd never dare disobey."

Dirck managed a lopsided grin. "What hit me, Mr. Court? My head feels as if a rock had bounced off it." He put up an exploring hand and winced when it found a bleeding goose egg.

"A crazy bargeman with a broken oar in his hand tried to split you wide open. If it's any consolation to you, your father just whaled the daylights out of him and tossed him in the canal to cool off. But you'd be out like a snuffed candle if a pretty little blonde hadn't tossed an egg that spoiled his aim." Court chuckled. "Gad, Tinker, that was worth the price of admission. I got here in time for the kill, but none of us saw that bargeman start to swing. By the time we did, it was too late to do you much good. We stood there just gaping when suddenly that egg came sailing through the air and smacked him over the eyes. It upset his plans considerably."

Twisting around to see if Mrs. Van Arsdalen was on the way back to her patient, he spotted Mr. Sylvester walking toward them, a girl by his side.

"By jove, Tinker, take a look. Here the girl comes now with Guy Sylvester."

Promptly disregarding earlier orders, Dirck shoved himself up on one elbow and squinted at the approaching pair.

"That's Maddy Brandt," he said slowly. "I thought it would be." He hesitated for a fraction of a second. "Did you call her *pretty,* Mr. Court?"

That young man nodded emphatically. "I certainly

did." He grinned at the boy on the grass. "Haven't got blinders on your good eye, have you, Tinker? Great Caesar, she shouldn't have bothered to save your skull after all; it's probably empty."

Laughing at Dirck's startled expression, he got off his knees to greet Maddy and Mr. Sylvester, quick to acknowledge his introduction with praise for the girl's fast thinking.

Maddy dimpled as she curtsied. "I didn't really think at all," she confessed. "I just had to have something to throw and these eggs were handy. Oh, Dirck, wasn't it lucky you taught me to throw a ball?"

"Came in kind of useful," the boy agreed. "Thanks, Maddy, for bothering." His voice was gruff, but he pulled himself up and tweaked a curl gently.

"Is this the way you stand guard, Mr. Van Voorhees?"

Margaretta Van Arsdalen, coming back to find her patient on his feet, was thoroughly indignant.

"Shoo, everyone of you, so I can work. No, not you, Maddy," as they started to turn sheepishly away, "you can stay right here and help. Besides," she drew the girl to her, "I want to thank you myself."

Court Van Voorhees turned on his most beguiling smile. "I'm practically groveling in the dust, Mrs. Van Arsdalen. What can I do to make amends?"

Margaretta laughed in spite of herself. "If you're going on into town, you might leave Maddy's eggs at the Queen for us. Dirck was going to take them, but he'll not get there this afternoon. Perhaps you'll explain to Staats; then he won't be wondering what's happened."

Dirck began a voluble protest, but his mother remained adamant.

"Here you are and here you stay until I see how much that head of yours is damaged. You can go tonight if you're all right."

"And maybe by that time, your face won't scare customers out of the place," Court consoled him. "Right now you're no asset to business."

Taking the eggs Maddy handed him, he strolled off, leaving Dirck's battered features to the thoroughgoing application of his mother's ointments and poultices.

CHAPTER NINE

Revenue Men

MARGARETTA VAN ARSDALEN looked contentedly at the group around the dinner table. Already, thanks to her salves, Dirck's face was healing. The bruises showed an ugly purple, but the swelling around his eye was going down, and the gash on the back of his head and the cut over his cheekbone had begun to mend. It would be awhile yet before he could smile with any degree of comfort; otherwise he seemed right as rain.

Certainly his spirits didn't need any doctoring. Noonday meals with Mr. Sylvester acted like a tonic on them. With quiet satisfaction Mrs. Van Arsdalen watched the engineer's interested response to Dirck's questions and noted her husband's alert participation in after-dinner discussions.

Mercy on me, she thought, listening to the rattle of talk, a few days more of this and I'll be trying to build a canal myself.

For a moment her mind wandered off to plans for supper, only to be drawn back by Dirck's voice asking Mr. Sylvester more questions.

"I keep thinking about those new barges, Mr. Sylvester," she heard him say. "They're pretty big, I know; maybe Sturdevandt's never will build any bigger than the *Alligator,* just as folks say, but twenty years ago nobody dreamed they'd float anything that size either. I can't see why they won't want to build larger and larger ones to carry more coal. Maybe I'm just crazy, sir, but I don't understand the canal company. Why doesn't it spend more money when it's spending so much anyway and widen the canal a lot? Wouldn't it be cheaper to do it now than get engineers in all over again later?"

Guy Sylvester gave him a keen glance. "That all your own idea, Tinker?"

"Yes, sir. I guess it's crazy all right, but it's bothered me until I had to ask."

"No, it's not crazy, Tinker," the engineer answered promptly. "It's sound good sense. A couple of the directors tried to make the rest see it that way, but they wouldn't listen. The *Alligator* is the final word to them."

He paused thoughtfully. "Their famous packet boat is outdated; couldn't compete with the railroads. Their freight barges can't compete forever either, not in speed at least, but, by George, they could compete in rates. Built big enough, they could carry coal so cheaply that mine owners couldn't afford to complain of slower transportation.

"Remember this, Tinker: it's an engineer's job to make special recommendations when he does his survey; afterward he carries out the decisions embodied in his employers' contract with him. I made my recommendations, but when they called me in for conference, I couldn't deny these current improvements would be ample now, maybe even for a considerable time to come. After that," he shrugged, "who knows? You and I could be wrong, lad. Anyway, the decision was the directors', and if they're satisfied, who are we to carp?"

Pushing back his chair, he rose reluctantly. "A dinner as good as that one deserves leisurely appreciation, Mrs. Van Arsdalen. I don't want to go back to work at all. By the way, if you don't need Tinker, I'll take him along to the outlet with me. There are a couple of papers I'd be obliged if he carried back to my quarters at the Queen as he goes."

Mrs. Van Arsdalen nodded cheerfully.

"That's a fine man, Jacobus," she said as the pair swung down the path. "There's no nonsense about him. He's no trouble at all."

She began to clear the table while Jacobus puffed at his pipe, apparently absorbed in some speculation of his own. Finally he roused and turned to her, a puzzled look in his eyes.

"Queer the boy should think ahead about the canal that way," he said slowly. "What's happened to our boys, Margaretta? First Pieter, now Dirck. What makes them act different from other Van Arsdalens?"

"Change is in the air, Jacobus." His wife's voice was gentle. "Pieter is very like you, but he's altered enough to suit another generation just the same. And they're both Van der Lindes as well as Van Arsdalens remember. We never had a chance to develop pioneer virtues; you Van Arsdalens had already built a town for us when we came.

But Grandfather Van der Linde built dikes, Jacobus. Perhaps Dirck isn't acting so very different after all."

She smiled up at her tall husband confidently. "They're not your sons for nothing, Jacobus. They'll wear off their rough edges and iron out their problems like all the Van Arsdalens before them, never fear."

Jacobus smiled back. "You're a comfortable woman, Margaretta. If it's Van der Linde sense they end up showing, I'll not complain, leastways not till it teaches them to twist me around their fingers like their mother."

Eyes twinkling again, the lockkeeper gave his wife an affectionate kiss and started off for the outlet. Left alone, she finished her chores to the accompaniment of her own gay soprano. Since the Lord helps those who help themselves, Margaretta Van Arsdalen wasn't going to be caught napping. After all, it never did a mite of harm to lend Providence a hand, and she'd managed all right about that business of having Mr. Sylvester for dinner. Obviously it had already accomplished something.

Contentedly she spread her dishcloths on the grass to bleach and picked up a wooden measure. Likely there'd still be first-crop beans down in the garden patch, and she might as well stroll down to pick them. Besides, she felt a few prickings of curiosity herself. Maybe if she watched a bit, she could figure out what made just widening a canal so exciting to her son.

She told him about it next morning at breakfast. "Mr. Sylvester says they are going to swing the new gates and haul out the breakwater posts today. Your father thinks they'll probably finish this whole section clear to Albany

Street in a couple of weeks if the dry weather lasts."

Dirck's face clouded at the thought, but his mother laughed at him.

"I wouldn't start worrying yet. They're here now, so be off with you and send your father in for breakfast." She chuckled. "Tending winch awhile will keep you right in the thick of things."

Dirck was still spelling his father at the locks and eagerly watching the final check of the big gates lying on the bank when he first sighted a cutter heading toward shore. She churned along at a brisk clip, the sun turning her wake into a kaleidescope of colors behind her. The Federal revenue fleet, based down at Amboy, patrolled the navigable waters for a good many miles around, and the Raritan carried its share of them.

Dirck shaded his eyes with his hand, trying to identify somebody in her crew. The sailor at the tiller was strange to him, but that was Captain Swenson standing beside him all right, so the cutter must be the *Kingfisher*. A few moments later she was standing by, close to the outlet, while a couple of men dropped over her rail onto the towpath.

Leaning against the winch shack, Dirck watched them cross the catwalk and turn toward him.

"We're looking for the lockkeeper, Jacobus Van Arsdalen. Any idea where we can find him, young man?" The older of the two, a man with gray hair and heavy features, addressed the boy.

"I'm his son Dirck, sir. Father's over at the house yonder having breakfast. He'll be back shortly, I expect—unless you'd rather step across and see him there." Glancing back at the house, he saw his father just leaving the kitchen door. "Here he comes now. You might as well wait."

Nodding agreement, the men tried to find a patch of shade. "Too hot to walk any farther than you have to these days. Heat fog's thick down in the bay. Weather gets worse daily. Gardens look sick, and wells are mighty low all up and down the river. We're heading straight for trouble when this spell breaks; it'll rain plenty."

They were fanning themselves with their hats when Jacobus came up beside them.

"Well, gentlemen," his voice was questioning, "anything I can do for you? You're off the cutter, I take it."

"Jim Malone and Laurent Arrie, Van Arsdalen." The older man, Arrie, showed their credentials. "Yes, we're revenue service. We think perhaps you can help us."

He glanced briefly at the workmen hard at preparations for hoisting the gates. Their own noise kept them safely out of earshot.

"New York's got wind of jewels being smuggled past customs. Two consignments have got by them and apparently been disposed of in Philadelphia. Now word's leaked out of a third likely to be landed within the week. Their operators are covering customs and the railroads. We're asked to take care of the water route. We can, and have, put men aboard the steamboats, but these freight barges are another story."

Mr. Van Arsdalen nodded soberly. "Hard to add a new man to some of their crews without rousing suspicion. A lot of them have worked the same barges for years. They're hotheaded enough to hunt trouble anywhere they can find it, but they're mostly honest. Your purse is as safe in their breeches as in your own."

Mr. Arrie agreed. "Checks with everything we know of them. But—and here's the meat of the matter as Malone and I see it—a couple of new barges have recently been added to the fleet. What do you know of their crews, Van Arsdalen?"

"Nothing good." Jacobus looked grim. "Rafters don't pull their punches, but they fight square. One of that outfit from the *Alligator* nearly split my son's head open with an oar pole the other day. Sneaked up behind him, mind you, in a free-for-all."

The lockkeeper's hands balled into fists as he talked about it.

"I'd never laid eyes on any of that crew on the river before Verne Giles signed them on. *Shark's* different; got a mixture: some new, some old, rivermen aboard her."

Mr. Malone and Mr. Arrie looked at each other. "Ten dollars say our men are on the new raft if they're on the river at all," Jim Malone sounded hopeful. "Jewels in a coal barge would be something new. Sounds like a slick crook somewhere at the top. Thanks, Van Arsdalen; we have an idea to work on anyway. Now if you can show us who's in charge of the canal job yonder, we'll try to get one of our men into his shore gangs. He might spot something when barges tie up for the night."

"Guy Sylvester's the engineer in charge; over there by the outlet, the tall, lean man with the mustache." The lockkeeper pointed him out. "And we'll keep our own eyes

84

open, the boy and I," he promised. "Naturally I was aiming to, after that ruckus the other day; now it goes double."

Dirck's eyes followed the revenue men until they reached Mr. Sylvester and drew him out of the crowd by the locks.

"They're talking to him now, Father," he said. "I know he'll help them out all right. Smuggled jewels in the coal! What a hiding place!"

"Don't let that idea run away with you," Jacobus advised him. "May be nothing in it at all. Normal course of events I'd laugh at it, but that crew on the *Alligator's* no good. Plain cutthroats is my opinion though."

"Maybe cutthroats and smugglers," Dirck suggested.

But his father wasn't ready to yield that easily.

"Likelier find a corpse than a diamond where they're operating," he growled. "Just beefy and mean. Not head enough for smuggling."

"But if there's a slick crook at the top, they wouldn't need brains; they'd just take orders. Besides, there's been a leak somewhere, and they're dumb enough to brag and feel big." Dirck was convincing himself fast at any rate.

"Plausible," Jacobus admitted. "But cutthroats or smugglers, it's all one to me. They're ornery mean, and I'll keep my eye on them."

He turned at a shout from the locks. The revenue men had gone, and Mr. Sylvester was beckoning to them.

"They're going to swing the gates!" Dirck forgot smugglers in a hurry. "Let's get over there and watch, Father."

"Release the winch crank first, son. They'll disconnect the cables on the old gates in a minute, but they may need slack to work them into place on the new."

Jacobus's order sent Dirck dashing into the shack, but he didn't lose any time he could help. He overtook his father in a second. Under the engineer's directions, workmen were slinging cable cradles around the new gates and running their guy ropes through pulleys on hoists.

"Winch crank's free," Mr. Van Arsdalen reported in answer to Guy Sylvester's question, and the engineer signaled his men to disconnect the old gates.

A demolition crew sprang into action as soon as they hung free. Pickaxes and sledge hammers tore against the wood, splitting and wrenching it into half a dozen bulky segments that were hauled speedily out of the way. Now water was slapping unhindered against the cedar-log breakwater, and Dirck could see how little seeped through. It had proved an effective device. In twenty minutes the old gates had vanished, and panting laborers, their muscles bulging, were guiding the new gates slowly over the banks as the hoists snorted into action lowering them into the water.

It seemed to Dirck that the gates had hardly touched the surface before tow mules were hitched up to the breakwater logs, and more men were digging down in the water and mud at their base. Loud shouts from their drivers set the beasts straining heavily forward, each team dragging a log an inch or two out of the sucking mud. Workmen grubbed again, and once more the mules drove doggedly ahead. This time the logs pulled further and easier. It might take half an hour to clear them all, Dirck calculated, but they were fairly started.

He turned his attention back to the new gates. They

looked so raw and bare after the moss-covered planks he was used to that he wondered how long it would take to weather the new construction work. Something as old as the covered Landing Bridge up the canal was going to make the fresh lumber along the banks seem ugly.

He looked around for Mr. Sylvester. Rule and spirit level in hand, the engineer was checking the set of his new gates. Apparently he was satisfied, for he smiled and gave orders to anchor the hinges and the cables that ran from the winch shack. Workmen were already slipping the hoisting cradles off both gates. Finally a triumphant yell from the mule drivers heralded the successful removal of the last breakwater log; the gates were ready for operation!

Jacobus Van Arsdalen smiled across at his son. "You might like to stand by the winch, eh, Dirck?"

Nodding enthusiastically, the boy raced for the shack. Surely if his father guessed how much he wanted to handle the new gates before anybody else, he'd understand about engineering pretty soon. His hopes danced jigs as he waited for a signal from the outlet. At last it came. Promptly he levered the winch crank back into place and pushed it forward, around and forward again and again. Lusty shouts down at the outlet told him the new gates were successfully open.

Mopping his excited face, he ran to the door for a look. His father and Mr. Sylvester were shaking hands vigorously, and the work crews were slapping each other on the back. Catching sight of Dirck in the doorway, the engineer waved happily and signed to close the gates again. When

Dirck looked up next, both his father and Mr. Sylvester were standing in the doorway watching him.

Mr. Van Arsdalen grinned. "Dinnertime, young man. Tell your mother we'll be along just as soon as we get a turn at this winch."

"The new gates work easier than the old, Father; just wait till you try them." Dirck's eyes shone. "Now I'm ordered off, you'll get a turn all right," he chuckled. "You couldn't be trying to shed me, could you?"

He glanced back as he started off, but both men were already too absorbed in operating the winch even to notice he'd left.

CHAPTER TEN

Dreams Crumble

DINNER HAD BEEN a gay meal eaten in a mood of celebration, and Dirck walked into the kitchen of the Queen with his spirits so high Mrs. Molenaer commented on it.

"You look as though you'd just lapped up a saucerful of cream, Tinker," she said promptly. "I'd send you out to tidy your whiskers on the back doorstep with tabby if Staats didn't want you to run an errand. He's behind his desk in the common room making out a list for you now."

She watched Dirck's springy step on his way to the innkeeper. "Good thing that boy's going out," she told Katje. "He's carrying too big a head of steam to be cooped up in this kitchen safely; might blow the roof off any minute."

From his seat at his desk, Mr. Barckaloe gave an absent-minded flap of the list that he was studying before he looked up with his usual broad smile.

"You don't look as though you'd mind a bit of exercise, young Tinker. By St. Nicholas, I'd go along with you if I didn't think this heat would melt the mutton tallow I'm made of nowadays. Watch out for Antje's cooking, my lad; one of us has got to keep spry around this inn."

He went over the list in his hand with the boy. "Now you've got that eye open, you can read it to Miller," he said, "unless, of course, you take on a barge crew or two along the way. Maybe I'm sending the wrong messenger up that towpath."

Dirck smiled crookedly. "I'm not hankering for more trouble this week, Mr. Barckaloe. I'm ducking behind the mules every time a barge passes. You want me to lug any of this stuff back from the grist mill, sir?"

"Only that small sack of buckwheat, Tinker. Tell Miller to send the rest of the stuff down the road by cart tomorrow. Antje will singe his whiskers if it's not on hand early. Tell him so; he moves fast, for Miller, where she's concerned."

The sun blazed hot on Dirck's back as he swung down Albany Street toward the Toll Bridge. People certainly weren't hurrying much. On the corner, the Town Crier leaned comfortably against a tree, glibly advertising a stock of religious books for sale at Abraham Ackerman's store on Burnet Street. The mob of small boys congregating around him rivaled the clamor of his bell. At the bridge Dirck climbed down the steps to the towpath and headed upstream. He had almost two miles to go, and he might as well make the most of it. He didn't get as far out of town as the Landing Bridge every day.

Frogs cherwunked along the canal, and gulls, flown inland from Raritan Bay, squalled in the wake of the shad fishers on the river. Leaning over the canal bank a moment, he watched a small bass streak for the shelter of the pilings, a pickerel in close pursuit. Dirck tossed a stone at the pickerel and it sheered off in a hurry. He hadn't had much time for fishing this year himself, but he knew he'd always remember this summer, even when he was old and had forgotten a lot of other things. Wrapping his happiness around him like a coat, he moved on, following the lazy curve of the path.

Finally, ahead of him at the bend, he glimpsed the grist mill and the bridge. The Landing Bridge always fascinated him; it had seen so much that had happened on the river: flatboats loaded with grain to be transferred aboard the anchored sloops waiting to sail to New York and even to England; merchants and travelers and soldiers, red-coated British and tattered Continentals, even Washington himself. Grandfather Van Arsdalen had loved to tell about Alexander Hamilton mounting cannon on a hill above the river to keep the British on the other side and cover Washington's retreat to Trenton. It gave Dirck a queer feeling to think that Grandfather Van Arsdalen was gone now, though the wooden bridge he'd watched abuilding still spanned the river.

The miller welcomed him just inside the door, joshing him good-naturedly when the dusty chaff set him sneezing so hard he couldn't give the Indian Queen's order until he'd retreated outside.

"I'll take the buckwheat along," he finally choked out, "but Mrs. Molenaer wants the rest of the stuff sent early tomorrow."

Dirck grinned surreptitiously at the mixture of alarm and admiration that came over the miller's face.

"She'll get it; she'll get it sure. That's one woman I

don't aim to cross. A piece of her mind is mighty indigestible."

He bustled back into the mill for the flour, and Dirck lounged contentedly on the bench beside the door, idly watching a string of tow mules plod down the path in his direction. He waved cheerfully to the driver. Then, suddenly tense, he studied the barge at the end of the lines. It was the *Alligator,* no mistake about that. She towed slowly with the load she carried, but even so, she'd pass before he got his flour, and he'd surely overtake her again on the way back to town. The idea wasn't particularly comforting.

On she came and he tried to identify the man who'd swung that oar. It wasn't hard. One of them, he noted with considerable satisfaction, wore the marks of his father's fists all over his face. Dirck was glad to get a look at him at last.

Wondering what kind of taunts might come his way, he braced himself to send back as good as he got, but a couple of the crew merely hailed him casually. The rest ignored him, except for the fellow with the bruises. He glared such ugly hate that Dirck felt cold all over. Then all at once, he was mad clear through. Springing to his feet, he stared defiantly back. He wanted to remember that man's face. Head high, he studied it feature by feature until the bargeman floated out of range.

"Father's right about that fellow anyway," he muttered angrily. "He'd as soon cut your throat as eat."

After that man, it was pleasant to find the easygoing miller at his side again with the buckwheat sack in his arms. Dirck signed for it promptly and strode off down the towpath. At the pace he'd set himself, he overtook the *Alligator* on the next curve. He didn't even turn his head to look at her, but he slowed his step at the young driver's cheerful "What's your hurry, Tinker?" as he hauled alongside the mules. He'd gone to school with Henrik Coenraad, and they fell easily into conversation. Henrik jerked his head back in the direction of the *Alligator*.

"Nice, friendly crew I'm hauling today," he said. "Picked them up at the lock this side of Bound Brook, and not even a catcall out of 'em yet. I hear they mixed it up with the engineer's workmen down at the outlet the other day." He glanced curiously at the purple splotches on Dirck's face. "Is it true the one called Heinie went for you with an oar?"

Dirck pricked up his ears. "Heinie?" he said. "Thanks for his name. It's true all right, and it's true Maddy Brandt plastered him in the eye with an egg, if you've heard that."

Henrik roared his delight, but he sobered quickly.

"Tell Maddy to keep out of his way then," he warned Dirck. "He's cussed mean. Van Wie caught him abusing a mule the other day; no reason for it, just nastiness. You know how Van feels about the mules. He's carrying a horsewhip regularly now, just waiting for an excuse to use it on that Heinie. Van says he wouldn't dirty his hands punching him."

"Making himself popular everywhere," Dirck grinned sarcastically. "If I wasn't leaving you in such good company, Rik, I'd hate worse to pull ahead, but you move too slow for Staats Barckaloe's taste."

He ducked his friend's careless punch and began to put the last mile behind him at a real clip.

The inn was busy by the time he handed her buckwheat over to Antje Molenaer and fell to work on his accumulated chores. Mr. Ten Eyck, coming in to supper with Mr. Sylvester, chatted a moment with Dirck, but the engineer seemed to have something burdensome on his mind. He was quietly friendly, but he didn't say much. After his gaiety at dinner, his sober silence puzzled the boy. Maybe he'd struck a snag in his work late in the afternoon.

"Step up to my room when you leave, will you, Tinker? I'll be in all evening."

Dirck nodded. "I won't forget, sir," he promised.

He wondered a bit from time to time, but it was well after nine before he finished tidying up and was free to report upstairs. The engineer was sitting at a table working on his reports when Dirck knocked and entered his room. He pushed his papers aside and pulled a chair forward.

"Sit down, Tinker," he said quietly. "I promised your mother I'd see you before you started home. It's not good news I'm carrying, lad. No, there's nothing wrong with her or your father," he added hastily in response to Dirck's frightened question. "It's your brother Pieter. He came upriver this afternoon pretty sick. Dr. Schureman says it's typhoid fever. I'm afraid that means a long siege, Tinker, but the doctor says your mother is a good nurse. In the excitement I forgot to ask her to dismiss me from her mind. Please tell her I return to dining at the Queen tomorrow but that she's to call on me if there's something I can do."

94

"I'll tell her, sir," Dirck answered dully. He looked dazed and stricken.

"Did Dr. Schureman—" he stopped and started again —"Did Dr. Schureman say he thought Pieter would get well?"

"He hopes so, Tinker," Mr. Sylvester said quietly, "but he'll be able to tell better in a day or two. Keep your chin up, lad; your family is counting on you."

Dirck straightened his shoulders. "Thank you for telling me, Mr. Sylvester. I guess I'd better be off."

The rest of the week had a nightmarish quality for the Van Arsdalens. Dr. Schureman came and went without saying much. Mrs. Van Arsdalen showed the strain of nursing and waiting and hoping, but she kept a smiling face for Dirck and Jacobus. People were kind. Mr. Sylvester stopped by daily to lend a hand where he could. Mrs. Molenaer sent Dirck home at night with loaves of fresh-baked bread and wedges of cheese. Once he even lugged half of a big baked ham. Maddy left bowls of dewy raspberries from the Brandt berry patch on the doorstep mornings, and twice Mr. Ten Eyck's Tim appeared with an armful of flowers and pots of chicken broth.

But by Friday Dirck was so worried over his mother's white face and his father's haggard look he asked to stay home to help. They wouldn't hear of it, however.

"When Pieter gets over this," Jacobus swallowed hard, "he won't be able to do much work for a spell. Your job at the Queen, son, might make the difference between finishing seminary or having to leave."

"I hadn't thought of that, Father," the boy's voice was

so low it was hard to hear. "I guess I can't afford to be away even for a week."

His mother's eyes were full of pity for the dreams that were tumbling about his head. "I'm afraid trouble always drives double harness, Dirck." Her hand on his shoulder was strong and comforting. "But with the Lord's help, we'll unseat him yet."

Dirck nodded, afraid to trust his voice again for a moment, and began collecting the garden tools from their rack in the corner of the kitchen.

"I'd better get to work on the cornpatch," he muttered. "This dry weather's been hard on the garden. Blow the horn, Mother, if you need me. I'll be listening."

For two hours he worked furiously, trying to root out his own misery with the crab grass he dug. His conscience rode him ragged.

"What kind of a fellow keeps thinking of himself when his brother's as sick as mine?" he asked himself scornfully. "If Pieter just gets well, nothing else matters."

He clung desperately to that thought all afternoon at the Queen and on through the evening. Pieter's condition hadn't changed much when he got home, but Dr. Schureman was staying on with his patient. He expected a crisis sometime in the night. Watching the suffering on his parents' faces, Dirck was close to complete despair by the time his mother insisted that he get to bed.

He rested fitfully at first, jerking upright every little while, fancying he'd heard his father call him. At last, toward morning, he slept heavily, one arm flung up over his head. Not even the hot sun streaming across his face roused him until his mother reluctantly shook his shoulder. He waked with a startled cry, frightened at what might have happened, but one look at her face comforted him.

"Be as quiet as you can," she whispered. "Your father and Pieter are both asleep." Suddenly the tears began to roll down her face. "He's better, Dirck; he's going to get well now."

Dropping to her knees, she buried her face in the pillow beside her son and cried from sheer relief. He patted her shoulder awkwardly, trying to think what to do. Then he climbed out of bed and picked her up bodily, putting her down in his place.

"Here you stay for a while," he insisted. "No arguments. I'll wake you in an hour. Get some sleep while I dress and go down to the outlet."

After her first protest, Mrs. Van Arsdalen gave in. Sliding hurriedly into his clothes, Dirck tiptoed back for a look before he headed downstairs.

How tired she looks, he thought in dismay. I hate having to wake her so soon. He stole a look in Pieter's room as he passed; his brother was thin and wasted, but he was sleeping peacefully, his face no longer flushed with fever. Quietly the boy crept down the stairs and through the kitchen. His father, still at the table where he'd sat all night, had slumped forward, dead to the world.

Dirck hurried down the path to the locks. Barges tied up for the night were ready to move, fussy tugs waiting for them beyond the outlet. Still others in a steady procession floated down the canal from above the Toll Bridge. Deep lock had already been opened. Quickly Dirck cranked the winch and set the gates wide. Standing in his father's customary place on the bank, he watched the rafters pole their barges out into the river. Men hailed him good-naturedly, some of them eating their morning bread and cheese as they drifted along, and he answered automatically.

Actually he hardly noticed what they called. Try as he would, he couldn't seem to get his tangled emotions straight. His relief at Pieter's escape was all mixed up with the cold, sick misery of his own bitter disappointment. Sighing, he tried to think things out. He wanted to help Pieter, of course, just as Pieter would help him if their positions were reversed. But not begrudging Pieter his wages didn't seem to make giving up his own plans any easier. If only he hadn't been stupid enough to build his hopes so high!

A few minutes later Maddy found him sitting on the bank staring unseeingly at the canal. The girl was frightened by the unhappiness in his face.

"Is Pieter worse?" she faltered.

Dirck's face brightened at once. "He's better, Maddy. He's going to get well."

Maddy felt bewildered. He was obviously happy about Pieter. Then what had made him look so miserable a minute ago?

Hesitating a little, Dirck began to speak again. "Of course, he won't be strong for a long time. Father thinks he won't be able to do any outside work this winter; just go to classes."

The girl was quiet a moment, watching him, trying to

feel her way. "You mean he'll need the money you earn at the Queen? You mean you won't get to go to Rutgers?"

Dirck nodded dumbly, his disappointment too deep for words.

Maddy's throat felt choked, and her eyes smarted with tears. Fiercely she blinked them back. This was no time for crying.

"Don't you dare give up, Dirck Van Arsdalen!" Her voice lashed across the boy's numb misery. "Last night Father was reading us a story about a poor pastor who had troubles come in heaps. But he never got really discouraged; he just kept telling his family to keep inflexible and fortune would turn in their favor. You'll have to be like that Vicar of Wakefield, Dirck Van Arsdalen. A little thing like this can't stop you. You'll be an engineer yet."

She waited a minute, but Dirck paid her no heed. She'd burst into tears if she stayed another second, and then he'd know how discouraged she was, too. Turning hastily, she fled across the field toward home where she could cry in peace.

Dirck lifted his head and watched her retreating back resentfully. "Much she knows about it," he muttered; "calling it 'a little thing like this.'"

He got heavily to his feet. He had to go back and wake his mother. No use adding to her distress by wearing a long face. At least at the house he wouldn't have Maddy coming around like Job's comforters. Resolutely he squared his shoulders and started back the path to the kitchen door.

CHAPTER ELEVEN

The Alligator Again

DIRCK WAS STILL arguing with himself next morning as he rowed steadily out midstream. It was easier to decide to forget all his dreams than it was to accomplish it. No matter how carefully he shoved the thought of Rutgers into a corner of his mind, it kept tumbling out to start the ache in the back of his throat all over again. Maybe out on the river he could think straight again.

Gradually the rhythm of his stroke relaxed his tense muscles, and some of the dull ache began to go. Shipping his oars, he drifted in the sun, his line trailing over the stern. Losing a couple of bites stirred him up a bit, and he started to concentrate on his bobber. It was queer how fishing helped a fellow forget. He stretched and settled down to business. With a little luck he'd take dinner home with him.

Suddenly alert, he hauled in his line to land a threshing shad in the boat beside him. Then he dropped two more in rapid succession into the basket in the bow. After that his run of luck turned. Patiently he picked up his oars and rowed further downstream. That did the trick. He was removing the hook from a fourth fish when he finally realized someone was making a lot of fuss in the distance.

Over on the shore his father was blasting away on the horn and waving energetically. Dirck signaled back, rewound his line, and began to row back to the outlet. The catch wasn't bad, he thought; anyway, it was plenty and to spare for dinner. He remembered idly that he never had kept his promise to take Maddy fishing after she'd picked those strawberries. One thing sure, it didn't worry him any, not after the way she'd talked. That just didn't make sense.

He wished angrily that he hadn't thought of her. Now in spite of himself, he was worrying again. He was glad he hadn't looked at her yesterday—though he hadn't needed to; he knew how her eyes could snap.

"Don't you dare get discouraged, Dirck Van Arsdalen! A little thing like this can't stop you." He could hear her saying it now.

First thing he knew, the words had got mixed in with the rhythm of his oars: "A little thing like this can't stop you" over and over. Annoyed, he changed his stroke, but there they were, back again: "A little thing like this can't stop you." He couldn't get rid of those words. Still, thinking about them out on the water this way made them sound different somehow. Maybe Maddy had just been trying to starch his backbone. Looking back, he began to suspect that she had managed plenty of times to get him to try again when something he'd tackled had gone all wrong.

But how could he help being discouraged? No matter what she said, giving up his savings and handing over his wages was not a little thing. What was that story she'd told him about? He tried to remember: something about a poor pastor down on his luck. Now that he knew enough not to get his hopes up, perhaps he'd get her to tell him more about that preacher. Beginning to whistle under his breath, Dirck bent to the oars and sent the boat skimming back to the locks.

His father was standing on the catwalk trying to mop his face dry as Dirck tied up.

"I began to think your ears had melted off out there," he said good-naturedly. "Town Crier claims they're frying eggs on the cobbles down Albany Street. Here, I'll take your fish along to the house with me, unless you think they cooked enough on the way in. It wouldn't hurt you any either to hug the shade while you spell me; you look half cooked yourself."

Mr. Van Arsdalen shook his head disgustedly. "You decide it couldn't get any hotter without the ground beginning to smoke; then the next day goes the one before a couple of degrees worse. Heat like this won't help Pieter much. Strained soup and hot weather! What a combination to fetch a fellow's strength back."

He picked up the basket of shad and marched off. Left alone, Dirck automatically checked the winch before he stretched out in the shadow of the shack where he could watch for signals from the flagmen. The heat was terrific. Overhead the sun was brassy. The air lay on him heavily like something dead and clammy. Along the river banks the red mud was cracked in hard, dry fissures. Mules, unhitched from the towlines of four barges tied up just above the outlet, cropped the browned grass half heart-edly, hardly bothering to switch the flies off their flanks. Some of the bargemen talking to Dirck shook their heads ominously over the crops burning up back country.

"It'll rain bad when this hot spell breaks," they told him. "Ground's so dry it won't soak it up either. The river'll rise, son. We'll be the lucky ones, floating."

The revenue men had said nearly the same thing over a week ago, Dirck remembered. Seeing workmen off in the distance climb up over the bank for their noonday meal, he wondered again which one might be the Federal man. As far as he'd been able to tell, they all looked like Mr. Sylvester's regulars. If he walked the towpath on the way to the Queen this afternoon, he'd get another chance to study them and see if he could guess. Mr. Sylvester had certainly forged ahead with the work this past week. Another two days should finish the new bank straight up to the Toll Bridge. A signalman up-canal dipped his flags, and Dirck pushed lazily to his feet. He wigwagged his arms a couple of times and ambled into the winch shack to close the outlet. A moment later his father appeared, ready to take over.

"Your mother needs some water as you pass the well, Dirck. I left the pails there for you when I came down." He looked a little anxious. "That well's getting all-fired low. It can't hold out much longer—though likely we'll have more water than we want when it does come," he finished soberly.

Dirck walked thoughtfully to the house for dinner. What the bargemen had said had gone in one ear and out the other. This was different. It wasn't like his father to worry. If he was apprehensive, weather was really brewing. Dirck began to wonder what did lie ahead.

Walking up the towpath later, he hunted signs of rain, but the sky was as cloudless as ever with the same heavy heat haze veiling it. Just the same, the air seemed thicker and more oppressive every minute. It made his head feel stuffy as though he were breathing in something that needed straining. He began to hope the Queen would be empty and he could get time off to finish the clock. That would be a cool job compared to dashing around for Mrs. Molenaer. Besides, he was nearly through; a free half-hour and he'd have the works back in the case. They'd been running fine all day yesterday, ticking away in perfect order.

He eyed the workmen curiously as he passed them strung out along the bank, but spotting the revenue man was beyond him. Then he saw the *Alligator* tied up near the Toll Bridge. Why on earth should a barge with a full load of coal be tied up at this hour with a regular night-time snubbing? Puzzled, he stopped and prowled around. Not a rafter of her crew in sight, and she was tied fore and aft. It looked as though Verne Giles meant to leave her where she was until the next day. Tugs aplenty were waiting downriver; he'd seen a dozen before he left home, so she wouldn't have any trouble joining a string for New York. It was too much for him.

At the Queen things were humming. Dirck whistled when he saw the crowded stable yard. If all those people were staying beyond dinnertime, steamboat passengers had better head straight to Keyworth's, for there'd be no use coming way across town tonight. Any hope he'd had for a half-hour to work on the clock went into the dustbin.

He poked his head cautiously into the kitchen, half expecting to see Antje Molenaer flying about like a distracted hen. Her orders were rattling like hailstones, but she didn't look the least bit flustered. A couple rattled in his direction, and he made promptly for the common room under instructions to clear tables and carry trays.

If I let my wits meander this afternoon, I'm likely to be out of a job before the day's over, he warned himself firmly.

Working his way around diners to the end of the room, the boy set to work stacking his tray with dishes from the farthest table. Just beyond it he suddenly discovered Verne Giles sitting by himself, a black scowl on his weather-beaten face.

He looks as though he could bite the *Alligator* in two, Dirck thought. I wonder what's happened to make him so mad?

Glancing back for a second on his way to the kitchen, he saw the captain lumber up and start for the street, apparently in pursuit of a man slouching past the window. A second later, from the back door, Dirck watched him overtake the man at the corner and spin him around. It was Heinie, no mistaking that ugly, sullen face. Hearing Captain Giles bellow angrily, Dirck waited for what might happen next. But Heinie only shrugged, and Verne Giles stumped furiously down to the river.

Whatever was wrong, the captain obviously hadn't

mended. It seemed as if trouble had signed on as a regular crewman aboard the *Alligator*. Dirck wished he knew what was going on. Feeling the way he did about those rafters, he'd be more comfortable if he knew what they were up to. He went back to work considerably worried, but as the afternoon churned by with a string of chores in its wake, he didn't have time to think.

CHAPTER TWELVE

A String of Rubies

AFTER THE RECORD crowd for dinner, half of Antje's staff was elbow deep in dishwater; the rest kept their fingers flying preparing supper. Dirck saw the kitchen himself only when he darted in for more cloths to wipe the common-room tables or brought back the broom. He felt all arms and legs trying to clean up like a ghost without disturbing guests who wanted to linger around to write letters and read the paper.

Just as he was giving a final polish to the last table, Mr. Sylvester came downstairs and strolled over to the innkeeper's desk. Evidently he had something on his mind, for he drew up a chair and settled down to talk to Mr. Barckaloe. Dirck heard them laughing as he hustled out to the kitchen to see what Antje Molenaer wanted next. He was about to dump the last pans of vegetable parings in the pigpens when Trina came flying down the back path from the inn.

"Mr. Barckaloe has come into the kitchen twice looking for you, Tinker. Mrs. Molenaer says to tell you to hurry back. Here, let me help you empty that pan."

Together they threw the parings to the squealing pigs

and, grabbing the pans, hurried up the path. Dirck was still wiping his hands on the towel someone had tossed him in the kitchen when he reached Mr. Barckaloe's desk.

"You wanted me, sir?"

The innkeeper nodded. "An errand for Mr. Sylvester. Meet the *John Neilson* at the dock, find Captain Frazee, and bring back the packet he'll give you. Here's Mr. Sylvester's note for the captain. Hold fast to it, mind, or you'll get no papers. And look sharp, Tinker; I need you back here. Send Jon along in from the stables as you go; he'll have to do till you return."

Dirck stuck the note in his pocket and started for the door.

"I'll be back just as soon as I find Captain Frazee," he said.

Stopping at the stables long enough to send Jon in to the Queen, the boy was soon zigzagging through Albany Street traffic and starting down Burnet. He looked down at his own long legs with approval. Maybe he didn't always know where to put them, but they were built to cover ground.

At Church Street he saw men strolling home from business and chatty groups of housewives filling pails at the town pump. Half past five was a pleasant time to walk through town, even if you had to hurry. With the day's work nearly ended, people acted easy and neighborly. Glancing up at the town clock in the Dutch Church tower a block westward, Dirck lengthened his stride. The *John Neilson* was due to dock at six, and he'd better be on hand to catch Captain Frazee as soon as the boat tied up, or Staats Barckaloe would have plenty to say.

Carriages began to roll by, their liveried coachmen intent on finding good places to wait for their masters sailing home from New York. A matched team of bays turned in from Liberty Street, and he recognized Mr. Ten Eyck's Tim on the carriage box. Plenty of people he knew waved from their stoops, but no one was visible at his own house when he neared the end of Burnet Street and saw the wharf ahead. He still had lots of time. Neither boat had come into sight, though beyond the curve at the river bluff two hovering columns of smoke announced their approach.

Down at the landing, people had chosen their favorites for the return run and were craning their necks to spot the first boat around the bend. Excitement ran high, and shouts of satisfaction roared up from Captain Frazee's backers as the *John Neilson* swept into view. A moment later the *Antelope* ploughed furiously into her wake.

Captain Van Wickel was obviously crowding on every ounce of steam, for his boat suddenly seemed to leap forward. A bargeman idling on the wharf let fly a string of oaths and began to shout. Somebody groaned, "He has no leeway, but he's trying to pass just the same."

It was true. In spite of the shallow, treacherous channel, Captain Van Wickel was maneuvering for a turn, and the *John Neilson* was being crowded toward the bank. The watchers on shore heard the frantic, warning blasts of her whistle and saw the scurrying figures of passengers and crew.

Now the *Antelope* attempted to swing wide. She hovered a moment and then churned obediently toward the farther shore. The frightened onlookers saw her bow run clear. But her forward speed was still terrific. Her stern cut in, grinding and splintering, to strike the *John Neilson* just aft of the paddle wheels.

Along the shore, rivermen scurried for their boats and headed for the stricken vessels. Late shad fishers put about and rowed hurriedly downstream. From the wharf Dirck could see his father cast off the moorings of a tug tied up below the outlet and jump down to join her crew as she chugged away. How he wished he could go along instead of standing here while people milled and shouted around him. Next thing someone would get knocked overboard, and there'd be more yelling.

Twisting and dodging, the boy inched forward to the pilings over the waterfront. Now at least his view was clear. Nobody on the river was paying much attention to the *Antelope*. Apparently she was hardly damaged. The impact of the collision had swung her stern clean about and free. Steaming noisily, she moved slowly upriver toward the dock.

But fishing boats were swarming around the *John Neilson*, and the solitary tug had heaved to alongside. Suddenly there was a scramble of small craft, hastily putting distance between themselves and the big steamboat. Her paddle wheels were moving again! Cautiously at first, then more confidently, she moved ahead, the tug staying close to her splintered side.

As she turned in for her landing, Dirck got a good look

at the damage. A whole section of her after railing had been carried away, and several lengths of planking close to the waterline were crushed in like so many eggshells. She was limping badly, but she had come into port under her own steam. The Napoleon Company would have to put the slower *New Philadelphia* on her run for a while, but they were lucky at that. Then getting a glimpse of Mr. Neilson and Mr. Corlear hurrying down the dock, Dirck shook his head.

I guess I wouldn't think much about luck if the *John Neilson* were my company's boat. I'd be just as furious as they look, he thought.

Passengers from both boats were coming down the gangplanks now. They all looked white and scared. Several of the *John Neilson's* passengers, knocked off their feet at the time of the collision, needed a steadying arm. Dirck saw Tim scanning the passengers anxiously. The old coachman seemed so worried that the boy slipped over to his side.

"Mr. Ten Eyck 'll be along in a minute, Tim. At least he's over there at the back of the deck, so he's all right anyway."

Tim drew a quavering breath. "Thank you, Master Tinker, sir. I don' see Mr. Nicholas and I'm sure afraid he's hurt."

"He looks fine, Tim. Wait where you are with the carriage, and I'll tell him where he can find you when he's ready. I've got to get aboard that boat myself."

Skirting the gangplank, Dirck pulled himself up on a piling and over the *John Neilson's* rail. He had to find those papers for Mr. Sylvester before Captain Frazee got involved explaining the collision to his owners. Keeping a sharp lookout for Mr. Ten Eyck to tell him about Tim, he started forward along the deck, only to bump into the man he wanted just outside the captain's door.

"We seem to meet regularly nowadays, Tinker," Mr. Ten Eyck laughed. "You pop up in unexpected places."

"I have to see the captain, sir, to get some papers for Mr. Sylvester, but I was looking for you, too. I promised Tim I'd tell you where he is. You'll find him on the left-hand side of the wharf."

"Thanks, Tinker; I'll be joining him soon. And now if you have to see Captain Frazee, we can go in together. He has a package to hand over to me, too."

Mr. Ten Eyck knocked and then ushered the boy in with him in response to a call. The captain had apparently just reached the cabin himself and was hunting out his log. He showed the strain of the last hour, but he greeted his guests cheerfully.

"Young Van Arsdalen, Captain." Mr. Ten Eyck presented Dirck. "He has a note for you. Tend to him first, please. I know he has to get back to work."

Captain Frazee glanced rapidly through Mr. Sylvester's letter. "So you're the messenger, eh? If you'll just sign here, lad, you can carry your packet right along." And taking a large envelope out of his pocket, he tossed it down on the table. "Now, Mr. Ten Eyck, I suppose you've come for your package, too."

Turning, he made for a small safe set high in the cabin wall. Dirck heard him gasp.

"The safe's open." The captain's voice was hoarse. "It's been tampered with!"

With a shaking hand, he indicated the door, slightly ajar, and running forward, Nicholas Ten Eyck threw it wide. The safe was quite empty. Captain Frazee's face turned ashen.

"It's gone, Mr. Ten Eyck. Your ruby necklace is stolen."

Dirck knew he would never forget Mr. Neilson's face when he reached the captain's office and learned of the second catastrophe that had struck their ship in a day. Each man was sure the theft was a professional job, for the safe had not been forced, and Captain Frazee was equally sure it had happened during the excitement of the collision when everyone had rushed on deck.

"Nearly everyone," Mr. Neilson emended grimly. "Someone obviously stayed below."

Wasn't there supposed to be a revenue man aboard the *John Neilson,* Dirck wondered? Where was he while all this was going on? Maybe a trained man could help. A little hesitantly, he broached the subject to Captain Frazee.

"Some revenue men who came down to the locks to tell Father about jewel smuggling said they were putting Federal men on the steamboats. Isn't there one aboard the *John Neilson,* sir?"

Mr. Ten Eyck and Mr. Neilson looked startled.

"What's this all about, Captain?" Mr. Neilson demanded. "Where is this revenue man?"

"I'm wondering myself," the captain said, frowning. "He signed on as purser's assistant, Mr. Neilson, hunting for some smuggled jewels they got wind of. Let's get Mr. Cornelius up here and find out what's happened to his young man."

He rang hurriedly for the purser, and a moment later Mr. Cornelius joined the group in the captain's cabin. Their grave faces warned him something serious was up, but he wasn't prepared for a theft of such magnitude.

"Young Hanson was in evidence up to the time of the collision, sir," he explained in answer to the captain's questions. "Since then I haven't laid eyes on him. If he saw anything out of the way, he may be following someone, of course. He warned me he'd slip off without notice if necessary, and I haven't given him much thought in all the excitement. I'll take a look around now, sir, and see if I can locate him."

The captain nodded. "Get on to it immediately, Mr. Cornelius, if you please."

"Suppose you take young Van Arsdalen along to help," Mr. Neilson suggested. "I take it, gentlemen, we'd prefer to keep this from the crew until we see at least if we can locate this revenue man?"

The others agreed at once. "Time enough to let this leak out after we've consulted Hanson," the captain said. "We'd better be guided by him."

Dirck followed the purser down the passageway. It was his first visit aboard the big steamboat and he was feeling lost.

"Open every door you come to, lad, and take a thorough look. Aboard ship you're bound to end up eventually just where you started." Mr. Cornelius was reassuringly matter-of-fact. "We'll separate here, but give a shout if you want me."

He strode off, and Dirck started forward, peering carefully in the men's washroom and searching through the lounge. He had worked his way well around the bow when he heard somebody coming at a run. Tensing his muscles, he got ready to make a flying leap. Maybe Mr. Cornelius had flushed the thief. But it was the purser himself who came racing down the deck, his face white.

"I've found Hanson," he panted. "Come give me a hand, quick."

Together they ran back along the deck and into a passageway near the ladies' lounge. Dirck saw a half-open door marked "Stores" and behind it, jackknifed into the small closet space, the crumpled body of the revenue man.

"He's alive," the purser answered Dirck's horror-stricken look, "but it's no thanks to the man who black-jacked him and shut him up in there. Not enough air in that place for a parrot. Lend a hand now and we'll lay him out here in the passageway. Gently does it, lad; he's hurt bad."

He wiped his streaming face. "Report to Captain Frazee while I mount guard. Tell him we need a doctor quick. Head across deck and forward to your right."

Dirck went off at a run that fetched him breathless to the captain's door. Too upset to wait for an answer to his knock, he burst into the room.

"The purser found Mr. Hanson, sir," he gasped, "shut up in the stores closet by the ladies' lounge. Mr. Cornelius says to tell you he needs a doctor right away."

Captain Frazee's chair clattered over backward as he sprang to his feet.

"Is he badly hurt, lad?" he asked gravely.

"I'm afraid so, sir," Dirck answered. "Blackjacked hard over the head, we think. I'll try to find Dr. Schureman, if you like, on my way back to Albany Street."

But Mr. Ten Eyck intervened before Captain Frazee could answer.

"Too slow, I'm afraid, Tinker. Tim's down below with the carriage. We'll fetch the doctor while the rest of you carry on here."

But on his way out he beckoned to Dirck. "Better let me set you down at the Queen, too, Tinker; Barckaloe will think you've run off from your job. Be back as soon as I can, Captain," and he was gone, Dirck at his side.

The boy rode back to the inn in a daze. Things had been happening too fast for clear-headed thinking. The collision was bad enough, but the theft of the necklace looked even blacker. And now this attack on the revenue man made the whole situation worse. It might be days before Mr. Hanson could tell his story and they'd know whether he'd seen the man who struck him down.

Passing the Toll Bridge, Dirck caught a momentary glimpse of the *Alligator's* dark bulk at the side of the canal. His heart began to hammer. Could there be any connection between the jewel theft on the *John Neilson* and this queer business of tying up the barge the revenue men distrusted? Tense and excited, he poured the whole story into Mr. Ten Eyck's ears.

That gentleman considered it carefully. "Your idea is

worth investigating, Tinker," he decided, "but keep some of this strange business to yourself. Not the theft, of course; you'll need to tell that story to explain why you're late, and there's no use trying to suppress the attack on Hanson. The *Neilson's* crew will know by now and it'll be all over town by morning. As soon as I've got Dr. Schureman back to the boat, I'll try to find Captain Giles. Anything that might give me a clue to my necklace is worth following up. And I'll let you know what develops, Tinker."

Tim pulled up briefly at the Queen, and Dirck jumped out. "Thanks for the ride, Mr. Ten Eyck. I hope you find out something useful. I'll be waiting to hear." Then he ran for the door, anxious to explain his long absence to the innkeeper.

In the common room, of course, conversation had centered on the ramming of The Napoleon Company's steamboat by the ship of a rival line. Those of the *John Neilson's* passengers present denounced the *Antelope's* handling in loud and violent language, and when someone suggested that the collision was deliberately engineered by the *Antelope's* captain, the inn was packed with dynamite. Dirck's return with the news of the stolen necklace set the place in a new uproar and released another flood of words.

Few men were more admired and respected in New Brunswick than Nicholas Ten Eyck, and the concern over his loss was genuine. Townsmen who had sailed with the *John Neilson* from New York were thoroughly indignant. Strangers from the boat were somewhat uneasy; they felt that they naturally came under suspicion. One dapper gentleman at the small round table under the clock was vociferous in his laments that the theft hadn't been discovered before the *John Neilson* docked.

"Had we all submitted to search then, we would feel more secure, gentlemen. As things stand," he shrugged eloquently, "no one quite trusts us and we can't quite trust each other. An unpleasant situation, and we can't remedy it."

Inwardly Dirck agreed with him. He might be carrying trays and running errands, but his mind was obsessed with the robbery. The *John Neilson's* crew were all old employes, sailors recruited from the town; they might tear a safe to pieces with a jimmy and dynamite, but none of them had the skill for a job like this one. No, somewhere among the passengers the answer was hidden. You heard of gamblers and crooks plying their trade on the Mississippi; why not on the Raritan when the stakes were so high?

CHAPTER THIRTEEN

Rain at Last

THE STORM BEGAN in the night. Dirck half
roused to a slate-gray morning with lashing sheets of rain
blotting out the river below his window. Drowsy and con-
fused, he was ready to roll over and go back to sleep when
a sad-voiced tow mule uttered a violent protest against the
weather. Obviously it was time to get up. His father and
mother were both ahead of him. He could hear his father's
deep-throated chuckle and the gay lilt back in his mother's
laugh again, now Pieter was going to get better.

Dirck lay still for just a moment more listening to their
voices. It gave a fellow a comfortable feeling of security
to live in a family like his where nobody bickered. Dirck
liked the way his mother's face glowed when she looked at
his father, just as though someone had lighted a candle
behind her eyes, he always thought.

Sliding out of bed, he groped for his clothes. Maybe it
was supposed to be morning, but it certainly looked like
night in his room. And the rain hadn't done anything to
the heat either as far as he could notice. He felt hotter
than ever, and his clothes stuck to him in damp patches.

Down in the kitchen, his mother had the lamps lighted

just as she did on winter mornings, only there wasn't anything about this morning to make you huddle close to the fire. When Mr. Van Arsdalen tried opening the back door, he had to slam it hurriedly shut.

"Just one thing likely to enjoy this weather: that's a shad," he grumbled good-naturedly as he wiped up the floor. "Bargemen look half drowned and the mules could do with gills. At least you won't be able to worry about our being cold, Margaretta."

Mrs. Van Arsdalen eyed him firmly. "If you're trying to avoid an onion poultice, Jacobus, it won't work. Wet skins and onion poultices go hand in hand."

"Where you're concerned they certainly do," her son agreed. "The Indians hereabouts used sweat baths, Mother, and we'll be sure to have those anyway," he suggested persuasively.

Jacobus chuckled. "Might as well give up, son. She'll win hands down. Just wrap yourself up in a tarpaulin and hope for the best."

They finished breakfast and struggled out in the storm. Huddled in sailcloth jackets, they threshed their way against the driving rain.

The wind can't seem to make up its mind, Dirck thought disgustedly. Veers around like a weather vane. Being a turtle would be mighty convenient; I'd be glad to pull my head in.

At the lock they sought shelter in the winch shack, taking turns in dashes to the barges which, despite the weather, floated in a steady stream through the feed-in and the outlet gates. Rafters headed downriver for Perth

Amboy and New York said they had ridden the storm all the way from the Delaware.

"Upriver branches filling up considerable," they told Jacobus. "You'll see the washouts from them coming this way soon unless the rain lets up: roots and branches aplenty."

Jacobus looked worried. The shallow channel of the Raritan was mighty troublesome when its dozens of tributary streams back country filled too heavily and poured fast into the river. No telling what might happen if the storm lasted several days, and present indications were all against a sudden break. With no rain at all for six weeks and the wind straight out of a blast furnace, it wasn't likely the weather would change until it blew cooler.

In fact, as the morning wore on, the visibility grew perceptibly poorer. The rain was a thick curtain muffling river and boats alike. It was easier to recognize voices than faces when the Van Arsdalens lent a hand at the locks. Jacobus finally took his stand on the edge of the bank, ignoring as best he could the storm sluicing over him. He knew he couldn't trust his eyes even the little distance to the shack, and he wanted no accidents to cope with this morning. Tugs with their tails of tows were still moving downstream, though more and more cautiously, but an increasing number of rafts were tying up to wait out the downpour in security.

Dirck sloshed his way to the Queen that afternoon through a ghost town shrouded in mist. Shoes and stockings buttoned securely under his jacket, he waded barefoot through the streams of water running over the plank walks along Burnet Street. The earth parched dry from the long drought refused to absorb the sudden deluge, and gutters were awash.

In the stable at the inn, Dirck saw the ostler and both his yard boys busy wiping down steaming horses. Envying the beasts, he dashed across the yard and into the kitchen, to stand dripping water over Antje Molenaer's tidy floor like something hauled straight out of Davy Jones's locker.

"Mercy on us, the lad's half drowned!" Mrs. Molenaer hustled into action, sending Trina flying for towels and Katje for the mop. Bundling Dirck into the corner by the stove, she hung up a banket for a screen and ordered him out of his soaking clothes.

"Rub yourself down, Tinker, and wrap up in that sheet on the chair while I find Staats Barckaloe. He can rout out a shirt and a pair of his own breeches."

A vision of himself in the innkeeper's breeches was something at which Dirck's imagination boggled. It wasn't length that bothered him; he and the innkeeper stood an even six feet one. But Dirck suspected he wouldn't be risking any money if he wagered that Staats Barckaloe weighed in at two hundred and twenty. By anybody's arithmetic that left sixty pounds the innkeeper's clothing covered that his own didn't have to worry about at all. Maybe Mrs. Molenaer had a coil of hemp handy and he could emerge tied in the middle like a sack of meal.

When she tossed the clothes in to him, Dirck's suspicions became certainties; at least he knew the worst. He might as well get it over with; he couldn't postpone appearing indefinitely. Out he popped, clutching the breeches with both hands, and Antje succumbed to such helpless laughter that Mr. Barckaloe stuck his head through the door to see what was going on. One look at Dirck was enough to set him off, too.

Wiping her eyes, Mrs. Molenaer finally fetched needle and thread and began to take tucks in strategic spots, but Dirck put no faith in those breeches until he'd done his own anchoring with a stout length of rope. Even after that, he checked the drying of his clothes on a line over the stove with a hopeful regularity that elicited chuckles from everyone.

Outside the storm worsened. The Queen was comfortably busy, however, with travelers who found the going too bad to warrant trying to reach their destinations. Some had set out from Newark in mere drizzles, to be overtaken by actual rain when they reached Elizabethtown, but none had encountered anything along the way to match the Raritan Valley's furious downpour.

A few hardy New Brunswickers began to drop in toward supper hour, but local custom was obviously destined to be small. Mr. Ten Eyck, true to his word, stopped by to tell Dirck about his interview with Verne Giles. He hadn't been able to locate the *Alligator's* captain at all till mid-afternoon, for, thoroughly disgruntled with his crew, Verne Giles had set out for Perth Amboy late the day before looking for replacements and had had a hard time getting back to town in the storm. When Mr. Ten Eyck questioned him about the tied-up barge, he had exploded.

"Dead drunk, every mother's son of them, except Heinie," he had growled indignantly. "Came aboard drunk at Bound Brook and got more useless every mile of the way."

At New Brunswick, he explained, there had been nothing for it but to tie up and let them sleep it off. They'd been shiftless and surly right along, but this was the first time they'd actually got out of control. Captain Giles intended it to be the last. They'd sail no more with him if he could help it.

Dirck felt discouraged. He had hoped for something that might give him a clue to the mystery of the necklace instead of this prosaic explanation.

"How's the revenue man, sir?" he asked anxiously. "Is he able to talk yet?"

"He's improving, Tinker," Mr. Ten Eyck answered. "Dr. Schureman let one of his superiors interview him this morning, but Hanson has no idea what his assailant looked like; never got a glimpse of the man. As a matter of fact, he must have come close to laying the thief by the heels; thought he heard someone in the passage and was hunting for him. He'd just opened that stores closet for a look when the blackjack got him. He's taking it hard, berating himself for his lack of caution."

"It was tough luck, sir; no wonder he feels badly." Dirck felt sorry for the revenue man's plight. "But it doesn't help you much, does it?"

Mr. Ten Eyck shrugged. "Not much," he agreed. "They'll keep on the job, of course, both the revenue service and Town Marshall Fitten. And I'll offer a reward. That's about all I can do, but they think it's worth trying."

He turned up his coat collar and prepared to leave,

stopping for a word with the innkeeper at the door. Dirck watched him sympathetically, then returned to his tasks.

From his place behind the trestle table, he recognized the dapper gentleman who had been so talkative about the theft the night before. Seated again at the round table under the clock, he was playing host to a lady and gentleman from Newark who had arrived earlier in the afternoon. Dirck remembered their names, Mr. and Mrs. Arent Coejemann, because Mr. Barckaloe had treated them with such deference. Afterward he had seen them chatting together in the common room over cups of tea.

The lady was so pretty that it would be hard to forget her. Dirck didn't know much about ladies' gowns, but anyone could tell that Mrs. Coejemann was very fashionable. Right now her smiles at her companions sparkled almost as much as her rings and her necklace. Evidently the dapper gentleman found her charming and her husband well worth listening to, for he was most attentive to them both.

From time to time, Dirck's glance came back to the three at the table close beside him. The dapper gentleman's hands began to fascinate him. He had never before seen such tapering, sensitive fingers on a man's hand or such delicate white skin. Perhaps this man was a musician; he had always heard their fingers were like that. A little later two new arrivals coming downstairs to supper recognized the Coejemanns delightedly and promptly strolled over to pay their respects. They needed little persuasion to join the three already seated, and Dirck found himself laying the extra places for the newcomers.

It was then that he heard the dapper gentleman introduced as Mr. George Farquhar, "only recently back from a business trip to London." So he was just another businessman. Dirck was disappointed; a musician would have been more interesting. Still, he couldn't help wondering about those hands. They didn't seem to belong to the kind of businessmen he knew.

Of course, he had to admit to himself, I haven't known very many, but Mr. Farquhar seems different somehow. He's not a bit like Mr. Ten Eyck or Mr. Neilson or Mr. Corlear. He's, the boy hesitated trying to find words to describe the man to himself, he's smooth and silky and he purrs when he talks. I don't think I'd like him very much.

Absorbed in his duties, Dirck forgot the people at the round table for a while, and when he thought of them next, they were leaving the common room and starting upstairs. For a moment the lamplight outlined Mrs. Coejemann's slight, graceful figure and flashed from the jewels at her wrists, around her neck, and at her ears. The boy noticed how Mr. Farquhar's eyes were fixed on her.

I guess he thinks she's lovely, too. I wonder if he's known the Coejemanns long? He acts as though he had, but they don't treat him exactly like an old friend.

Shrugging the departed diners from his mind, Dirck went back to his trays and clearing. A few people were settling down to an evening of talk and pipes, but more left for their rooms, apparently counting on a long night's sleep and an early start in the morning. Peering for a minute out the back door, Dirck knew they were going to be disappointed if they really hoped for better traveling next day. The night, black as a coal pocket, was still lashed relentlessly by rain, and the wind had settled to a steady weather breeder straight from the southeast. Dirck began to laugh as he glanced up at his clothes now almost dry over the stove.

"They're going to be all ready just in time for another soaking, Mrs. Molenaer. The way the weather's acting, maybe this new uniform I'm wearing will get to be permanent."

Antje smiled broadly. "Don't trouble your head about those breeches again, Tinker. With all the water sloshing down you'll be wearing web feet and feathers tomorrow. It wouldn't surprise me if the feathers sprouted on your way home."

CHAPTER FOURTEEN

Flood!

DIRCK RECALLED Mrs. Molenaer's comment often next day as he splashed from one chore to another. The garden didn't bear looking at; his young corn was battered and twisted, and the peas and beans were a sodden mess. Maybe he could salvage some of it later, but, right now, digging it under and planting a late crop looked a sight more efficient. If he judged from the stuff floating down-river, a lot of other people's gardens on the banks had already been washed clean out. Cornstalks and yellow squash, even whole tomato plants, were sailing out mid-stream or bumping along the curving banks. The river carried a hodgepodge of debris from the upper reaches, too: all sorts of dead branches and stumps and battered planks. Once a small bridge, still nearly intact, caught on the wooden abutment of the outlet. Dirck got a half hitch around one end and hauled it ashore. Perhaps someone upriver would come looking for it; if not, it would make good firewood.

River traffic was nearly at a standstill. The steamboats made their scheduled runs, but passengers were scarce. Produce boats rode high in the water, their loads light, for truck farmers could neither pick nor cart their vege-tables safely. A handful of intrepid bargemen came down the canal during the morning to have their loads of coal taken in tow by waiting tugs, but Jacobus Van Arsdalen found his duties few. Together he and Dirck walked up the canal bank for a quarter mile. The rise in the river was perceptible now, the water lapping closer to the tow-path level.

"If this lasts another day, there'll be no holding her," Jacobus muttered. "Burnet Street will be clear under."

Dirck nodded. He had a dim memory of an earlier over-flow when the Raritan on the rampage had battered its way into town, but he couldn't remember any rain like this before.

"There hasn't been one in your time," his father told him. "Last storm anything like it nearly washed us out a month or two before you were born. Better tell Barckaloe not to expect you tomorrow if it's still raining. There'll be evacuation work for every able-bodied man—and woman, too," he ended grimly.

"I'll tell him," his son promised. "If travel's as light by road as it is on the canal, he can spare me fine."

Luck was with Dirck as he started for the Queen later. A peddler, driving his wagon along Burnet Street in search of a sheltering stable, offered the boy a ride. He climbed up beside the driver thankfully and tucked a big bundle wrapped in tarpaulin under the wagon cover with such evident satisfaction that the peddler grew suspicious.

"Kinda choice of that bundle, young fellow," he re-marked. "You mightn't be running away from home now, might you, and toting all your worldly goods?"

Dirck laughed. "They're worldly goods all right, Peddler, but I'm not running away. I'm just trying to keep them dry till I get to the Indian Queen. Yesterday I had to wear the innkeeper's breeches; today I'm going to wear my own, thanks to you and that tarpaulin. Perhaps the ostler would let you stay in the stable there if you were to ask him. He'll not likely be overcrowded weather like this."

The peddler chirked up immediately, urging his weary horse to a trot down to Albany Street. That usually busy highway carried a mere fistful of traffic today. Only a couple of wagons jolted across the Toll Bridge, and carriage travel seemed nearly nonexistent. The Town Crier, drenched and disgusted, was making the best of a sorry job, darting into taverns and shops to reel off his notices whenever he could find an excuse. They heard him crying Mr. Ten Eyck's reward for the recovery of the rubies as they turned into the inn yard. The Queen's stable had had no new arrivals since yesterday, Dirck noticed.

With hearty thanks to the peddler, the boy left him bargaining with the ostler and ran for the inn himself, his tarpaulin clutched in his arms. His bump of vanity wasn't especially large, but he was taking considerable satisfaction in the safe transportation of those breeches. He'd got them to the inn dry, and there they were going to stay to use, still good and dry, until the downpour was over. He wasn't as perfect an imitation of a water rat now as he had been yesterday, but it would feel good to climb into drier clothes. His breeches had blotted up a sizeable puddle from the seat of the peddler's cart. Antje and Trina chuckled at Dirck's triumphant expression as he unrolled his dry clothes and darted into the scullery to change.

"Practically no room for expansion in those breeches." Antje shook her head sadly when he reappeared. "He'll not be able to eat tonight, Trina; no space at all to take on food. Just like that fashionable gentleman inside; clothes cut so tight he has to peck like a bird to save his waistline."

Heading for the common room, Dirck smiled back at her over his shoulder. "But you might put an extra chicken on in case I lose weight between now and supper. You don't want to have to take reefs in these breeches right at the busiest time."

In the common room guests were lounging around casually, reading the local paper or sipping chocolate while they chatted. A few stood discontentedly at the windows watching the rain, but most of them seemed to be making the best of their enforced stay. Comfortable and dry and well-fed, they thought of some of the inns in which they might have had to take refuge and settled cheerfully in their chairs.

Dirck noticed Mr. Farquhar, as natty and dapper as ever, being affable to everyone. Seeing the close cut of his pantaloons, the boy thought of Mrs. Molenaer's strictures.

Guess he's the fashionable gentleman who pecks at his food, he thought. If he doesn't mend his appetite at supper, she'll have him marked for some bad end.

Strolling over to Mr. Barckaloe's desk, he remembered his father's warning about working next day. The inn-keeper listened attentively and nodded his head.

"I'll not expect you, Tinker, if the storm lasts. Matter of fact, I half expected real trouble today. We'll be all right here if the water doesn't back up Burnet Street too far, but the people down there will need all the help they can get. Some of our guests may get a little excited I'm afraid, but I can count on Mr. Sylvester and Mr. Coejemann to help calm them down."

"How about Mr. Farquhar, sir? He seems to be making friends with everybody; maybe he'd help."

The innkeeper snorted. "He's too much the fine gentleman, Tinker, to risk wetting his clothes if it comes to action. I can rely on him to support a lady on each arm; anything more strenuous might disturb the set of his cuffs."

Dirck couldn't help grinning. "He's not overpopular with Mrs. Molenaer either, sir. His appetite doesn't suit."

Staats Barckaloe laughed and shrugged. "Oh well, come the end of the storm and we'll see the last of him. He gabs all day like a female at a tea party and has less to say. I'll be glad to be shut of him. There's Mr. Sylvester coming downstairs now. Give him my compliments, lad, and invite him to join me. Maybe I can get a word in edgewise about the storm before our fashion plate leeches onto him."

Leaving the landlord and the engineer together, Dirck retreated to the kitchen and his chores. He knew Mr. Barckaloe would expect him to do as much as he could, for the likelihood of his being on hand next day was increasingly doubtful. He thought the wind blew a bit cooler now, the first encouraging sign the weather had given, but the rain poured down as steadily as ever. By this time he should be used to paddling around all day like a duck, but ducks didn't get onions clapped on their throats every night just because their feet were wet. A couple more days like this and his mother would have Mrs. Molenaer peeling him for a stew.

Polishing rags in hand, he shined pewter and copper until they looked mellow and then tackled the stove, buffing its brass and blacking its surface before he built a fresh fire for supper. It felt good to have the stove out even temporarily; cooled the kitchen a degree or two anyway.

His mind roamed away from the Queen. What would they do about Pieter if the river did flood? A sick person in a house half full of water got lung fever. The rest of them could make out on the second floor, but not Pieter. Maybe he'd stay dry at the Brandts if they could figure out a safe way to get him there. Maddy wouldn't mind waiting on him.

Dirck began thinking about the Vicar of Wakefield again. Maddy had told him the whole story when he cut across to see her in between chores that morning. She didn't ask any silly questions either or go fussing over him like a hen the way most girls would. And Mr. Court was right: she really was pretty. He'd been noticing. He'd been all wrong getting mad at her like that.

Trina's voice saying something about the Coejemanns jerked him back to the kitchen.

"Her husband's a jeweler, Mrs. Coejemann told me. No wonder she wears such beautiful rings. I'd be afraid to travel around with all those things, wouldn't you, Mrs. Molenaer? Mr. Barckaloe says her diamond necklace is worth a fortune, but she left it around just anywhere until

I told her how Mr. Ten Eyck's rubies were stolen and how everybody thought a professional thief was prowling about. Now she's wearing it all the time."

"It's safer on her neck than anywhere else," Antje agreed, "but if Mr. Ten Eyck's thief should still be around, it would be a terrible temptation."

"Mr. Coejemann thinks the thief would be afraid to try a second robbery so soon after the first, even if he is still in New Brunswick, but just the same, you should have heard him scold her for leaving her bracelets on the bureau when she went down to supper! He came back for her fan and found them there. That Mr. Farquhar was quite shocked. He said it was really unchristian to put such temptation in the way of the weak!"

Mrs. Molenaer eyed Trina severely. "You seem to have heard considerable, my girl. You wouldn't have been listening on purpose, I suppose, at least not if you value your post at the Queen."

"Oh Mrs. Molenaer, not ever! I could take my Bible oath, indeed I could." Trina was near to tears. "They stood outside their door and talked when I was washing the floor right beside them. I couldn't help hearing, ma'am, and that's the truth."

Antje relented enough to reassure the crestfallen girl, but she had no intention of letting her staff forget that she didn't approve of slack, prying maids. News was information that would help satisfy a guest's tastes or interests, gossip was just loose talk, and Trina had better remember the distinction.

Dirck had a strong notion that he had better remember,

too. Long ago Maddy had taught him that silence was golden when her Aunt Antje began to sound like a schoolmaster. Obviously this was no time for him to put his oar in, much as he'd like to say a few things about Mr. Farquhar. That man was a riddle and no mistake: his clothes and his manners made him out a regular dandy, and yet, according to Trina's story, he talked like a preacher. Dirck wished he could tell Pieter about him; Pieter always managed to make sense out of people when they just puzzled him. That's why Pieter was going to make such a good minister; he'd almost always know what made the people in his church act the way they did.

The boy thought of Mr. Farquhar again when he fought his way home through the rain. Tomorrow the man might have a chance to show what he really was, for trouble was certainly brewing fast. Even over the wind he could hear the rush of the river and the ominous slap of the water against its low bank. At the door of their house he met his father coming back from the locks, a lantern in his hand.

"I've opened the gates," he said. "It seemed the best course. At least Pieter will stay dry. Dr. Schureman came over and carted him off to his house."

There was a catch in Jacobus Van Arsdalen's voice. "He's so thin, it was like carrying a feather. Your mother's been moving preserves and vegetables out of the root cellar. Get into dry clothes as soon as you can, and we'll finish the job for her. She's done enough already, and there's a side of bacon too heavy for her anyway."

The kitchen was bright and welcoming in the lamplight. If Mrs. Van Arsdalen was worried over the rising water, she didn't show it as she stirred a pot of chocolate and toasted slices of coffee cake at the stove. Having Pieter safely cared for beyond the danger zone had removed her major anxiety.

"Dry clothes for both of you and a bite to eat before you do any more work," she said firmly.

Jacobus smiled at her. "No mutiny on those orders. That coffee cake smells so good we'll be back before you miss us. Coming, Dirck?"

Together they saluted smartly and hurried off, followed by the cheerful sound of Margaretta Van Arsdalen's laugh. Dry and comfortable again, they relaxed contentedly while they ate. Jacobus had news of doings along Burnet Street. Johann Brandt had stopped on his way home to report that stores were carting stock to higher ground on Neilson Street, and families were emptying their cellars of food and moving furniture to upper stories. Women had been down on their knees all afternoon taking up carpets and packing household treasures in chests that could be lugged upstairs. Now the street looked to be in a state of siege with the first-floor shutters closely barred and bags of sand piled around foundations, wherever people had managed to get hold of any.

Some folks had already dragged their rowboats across their yards and made them fast to pegs on their back stoops. Dirck nodded. He had seen a boat or two fastened to hitching posts as he walked home. They had given him a queer feeling in the pit of his stomach in spite of their looking so silly high and dry on the plank walks.

Refreshed by their bit of food and rest, he and his father

finished carrying the last loads out of the cellar while Mrs. Van Arsdalen tidied up. Dish towel in hand, she surveyed her kitchen's shining order and sighed.

Floods wouldn't be so bad if they just picked up after themselves, she thought. The next time we come out here we may have to wade through red mud, and a whole roomful of wet sugar wouldn't be half as messy.

She lighted candles for them all and led the way upstairs. They had done everything they could for the time being. It was wise to snatch some sleep in preparation for whatever the morning might bring.

To Dirck it seemed that he had hardly begun to doze when his father's urgent hand shook his shoulder. "Wake up, lad, wake up. The river's over the bank and rising fast. Into your clothes quick."

His words chased sleep as effectively as a pail of ice water. The boy's feet were on the floor almost before his eyes were open. Morning light filtered through the dismal rain outside his window, but it was still too early even for the lockkeeper to be stirring normally. Throwing his clothes on in a hurry, Dirck pelted downstairs to join his father in the kitchen. His mother was already there, with a pot of tea brewing and rolls warmed and buttered.

Everything seemed just as it had when they went to bed until he looked out the back door. Then he began to marvel that they were snug and dry and that the red mud his mother hated wasn't seeping over the floor. Everywhere he looked, water covered the meadows. The towpath had completely vanished under a swirling tide that raced inland and poured back toward the town.

Yet, by some quirk of fortune, they weren't entirely surrounded; below them southward the fields were still partly free. From their front windows he could even see the path to the street and the Brandt house, which, so far, sat well beyond the water line. As he dashed back to the kitchen, he heard his father's voice raised in determination.

"We can't leave you here alone, Margaretta, when there's no telling what time we'll get back. 'Twould worry us out of our wits. Dump the fire and pack some food; we'll row you to Brandts's."

"No need to row in that direction yet, Father," Dirck called. "I'll take Mother and the food across to Brandts's and bring Mr. Brandt back with me. That'll leave a boat there if the women need it later."

Helping his mother pack two baskets of food took more time than he wanted to lose, and he hurried her a little as they started across the path. With the water still rising, he didn't want to be caught midway on his return. Anyway he wouldn't have to worry about his mother once he left her at Brandts's, for he could see Maddy checking the painter on their dory right now. Apparently Johann Brandt had thought well enough of other folks' precautions to haul his own boat across the meadow to the house last night.

Seeing them coming, Maddy waited in the doorway to usher Mrs. Van Arsdalen in to dry by the fire and to help Dirck with the baskets. A moment more and he was ready to set out again.

"Take good care of yourself and your father," his mother ordered as he kissed her at the door

"I will," he assured her, "and if you have to use the boat, let Maddy handle it. There's no one on the river who pulls a better oar. Mind, young'un, you're skipper, no one else."

He smiled confidently at Maddy and was off to join her father on the path. The girl stood stock-still looking after him, astonishment and delight chasing so rapidly across her face that both mothers fell to laughing. Suddenly she found her voice.

"Oh, Mrs. Van Arsdalen, whatever is wrong with Dirck? He's never, never before said I did anything really well except bother him!"

CHAPTER FIFTEEN

Patrol Duty

THE RIVER WAS lapping fast across the southerly meadows as Mr. Brandt and Dirck started back to the Van Arsdalen house. After one startled look, they broke into a dogtrot and then into an outright run. But the river won: they were wading knee deep before they reached the front door and scrambled through. Jacobus hailed them from the second floor. Certain now that the house would be flooded, he had been lugging chairs and cooking utensils upstairs to join the supplies from the root cellar already stowed away in odd corners. With two more pairs of hands at work helping him, the lockkeeper soon had the first floor empty.

"What about your place, Johann?" he asked. "Hadn't we better shift things over there, too?"

Mr. Brandt hesitated a moment and then shook his head.

"I still think we're going to be all right," he said slowly. "The cellar'll flood, of course, but that's empty already. We'll be marooned sure as fate, and maybe we'll get some seepage, but the house sets so high I'm counting on that for protection."

Mr. Van Arsdalen was inclined to agree. "You're probably right. Anyway, the water won't wash through the way it will here. We'll row clear through this floor before the day's out, I'm afraid."

Pulling their jacket collars high about their necks, they took a final survey of the empty rooms and stepped out on the back stoop. With the water already rushing up over the steps, none of them doubted the truth of the lockkeeper's prediction. It was only a matter of minutes now before water would be battering against the kitchen door and slipping under the sill. Jacobus Van Arsdalen shut the door with some misgivings.

"Hardly know whether to close it or not," he muttered. "Might be better to leave both doors open and let the water wash in and out."

"Only you know it isn't going to wash out, Jacobus," Mr. Brandt said grimly. "It's going to stay until it reaches high level. Better shut out all you can."

They climbed into the boat and rowed across the fields down Burnet Street toward the heart of town. Everywhere they looked, the Raritan had wrought destruction. Here and there an iron handrail still protruded above the flood waters, but for the most part, shops and houses on both sides of the street seemed to be swimming in the river. On the lowest levels where marshlands offered no resistance to the onrushing tides, water was already pounding against barred first-floor shutters and the tops of doorways.

A weird collection of debris floated by them, swirling on the turbulent stream: chicken coops, doghouses, wooden washtubs, even a crate of eggs. Twice Dirck spotted a butter churn and a kitchen chair. Once a mahogany table sailed past, circling crazily as it struck heavier currents and then rushing forward again.

Rescue patrols in boats had begun to congregate at the Sturdevandt shipyards where Looe Sturdevandt and Town Marshall Fitten were taking charge. Under their direction, boats were being assigned to each block and setting out to pick up marooned families. Jacobus headed his dory in with the rest to await instructions. A few minutes more and he was rowing toward Hiram Street with orders to evacuate the Vredenburgs and the De Graws if they needed help.

This time, struggling back against the racing water, rowing was slow work. Mr. Van Arsdalen was winded when they finally turned up Hiram and hove to alongside the Vredenburg house. Dirck's shout brought little Engeltje Vredenburg and her mother to a front window. The child was obviously enjoying the excitement. It hadn't occurred to her to be frightened, and she clapped her hands in glee every time she saw a boat row down the streets where she usually played. Mrs. Vredenburg was thoroughly unhappy, however.

"We're the only ones home," she called. "Arie and Tunis went downriver trading before the storm broke. You can't get us out of here fast enough to suit me." Suddenly she looked down at the rowboat in dismay. "But how you think you'll get us into that horrible dory, Jacobus Van Arsdalen, I declare I don't know!"

The lockkeeper laughed. "I don't yet either," he admitted, "but now we're here I aim to find some way. If you'll just stand out of that window and let Dirck come aboard, maybe he can figure out a plan."

Standing cautiously erect while his father and Mr. Brandt steadied the boat, Dirck got a handhold on a jutting cornice. Apparently he was going to have to imitate a fly. Gingerly he inched his way upward, resting his toes on the narrow stone ledges and clinging to the ornamental ironwork with his hands until he touched the window sill and hauled himself over.

With Engeltje trotting at his heels, he took a quick survey of the stairway and the water on the first floor. Sending the child back to her mother for safety, he ran down and stepped out into water halfway up his thighs. From room to room he waded until finally in the back he found a window set high enough in the wall to be above flood level. He pushed it up and knocked energetically against the heavy shutters. Mr. Van Arsdalen promptly brought the boat around back.

"I can get them both out this way," Dirck called as soon as he heard the boat outside, "if you think it's safe to open this shutter. We'll have to lower them from that front window upstairs otherwise."

Mr. Van Arsdalen tapped with the end of an oar. "Water just about level with the bottom of the sill here, son. If you can get them onto the ledge, they can step up into the dory all right. We'll slop some water inside sure, but maybe not enough to hurt."

Dirck laughed as he pushed the shutters wide. "Take a look yourselves," he invited them. "Another gallon or two won't hurt a bit."

His father grinned at him. "How do you figure to get Katrinka Vredenburg through that lake?" he inquired interestedly. "She likes water just the way a cat does; nearly took a fit one day when she saw Johann teaching Maddy to swim."

"Piggy back," Dirck grinned back at him. "I calculate I can carry her weight just about that far."

He waved and vanished in the direction of the hall. Outside, the men could hear him splash through the first floor and then run up the stairs. A few minutes later he was back with Engeltje riding happily on his shoulders.

"Here's the first passenger," he called cheerfully, setting the child on the window ledge. "Over you go now, young lady."

He steadied her on the sill until Mr. Brandt lifted her safely into the dory; then he waded off again.

"He won't be back so fast this time." Mr. Brandt reached in his pocket for his tobacco pouch. "We'll have time to stuff our pipes." Listening for sounds from the house, he jerked his head discreetly toward the window. "I hope the boy doesn't have trouble, Jacobus; she's difficult if things don't go to suit her."

Up on the second floor Dirck was finding that out for himself. Mrs. Vredenburg had taken one look at the water in the hall and climbed heavily back up the stairs, berating him soundly for not thinking of a better plan. The boy hung onto his patience with both hands.

"You won't get wet," he argued; "not if you hook your feet around my waist and hang onto my neck. Maybe I could lower you out that front window, but I hate to try.

If I lost my grip, you'd swamp the boat, and everybody'd get a ducking. It's stay here or get out now, Mrs. Vredenburg. The water's rising so fast we can't use that window much longer."

Reluctantly Mrs. Vredenburg yielded. She'd been marooned long enough. The prospect of higher water made up her mind. Shutting her eyes tight as soon as they reached the lower part of the stairs, she climbed onto Dirck's back and clung frantically, fussing at every step he lurched forward.

About two more words out of her, and I'll buck her over my head, the boy thought indignantly. Anybody'd think I started this flood on purpose to annoy her.

He began to wonder if he'd ever be able to straighten his back again. Only the thought of the splash she'd make if he did toss her off buoyed him up for the last few feet. Peering in at the window, Mr. Brandt leaned hastily down to help Dirck transfer his burden to the sill.

"No call to strangle the boy, Katrinka." His voice was tart enough to make Mrs. Vredenburg open her eyes in a hurry. "And you'll sit on that ledge till the water washes you off if you don't help yourself. I'm not going to capsize us all lifting you off, and that's final."

Mr. Van Arsdalen smothered a grin and listened, fascinated, to the avalanche of furious words pouring over his friend's head. Mr. Brandt, however, remained unperturbed. He smoked placidly while the tirade lasted; then he knocked out his pipe and reached out a hand.

"If you've any breath left, Katrinka, maybe you're ready to come aboard," he said calmly.

146

Mrs. Vredenburg's face was still slightly purple as she wobbled to her feet and stepped into the dory, but she was quiet enough to suit anyone.

"Better close up that window on the second floor," Jacobus told his son. "We'll be back to pick you up as soon as we land our passengers near Neilson Street."

Backing the dory off, he pulled out of sight around the house, and Dirck started for the stairs again. Wet and tired, he was glad of a chance to catch his breath. Anyway he didn't want any more of Mrs. Vredenburg. He'd heard a bargeman's wife scold like that once when he was little and it had scared him stiff. He'd never forgotten it. He took a look out of the upstairs window: rain was still coming down in driving sheets just as if there wasn't water to spare all over the place. He was scanning the clouds for any possible break when Mr. Sylvester hailed him from a rowboat out front.

"Marooned, shipmate?" he shouted cheerfully. "Come on down and I'll take you off. Your father says no one's at home at De Graw's, but a shutter needs fastening. Where can I pick you up?"

"Round back, sir," Dirck called; "I'll be right down."

Shutting the window hurriedly, he ran downstairs to wade over to the back window again. He could hear Mr. Sylvester's boat bumping against the corner of the house as he climbed onto the sill. A moment later he was in the dory and reaching over to pull the window shut.

"Too bad I can't put the inside bar on these shutters," he said. "They'll stay latched all right enough, but they're awfully easy to open from the outside, Mr. Sylvester."

"No use stewing over it, Tinker," the engineer consoled him. "Most of the houses down these streets will have one shutter unbarred. It can't be helped when we have to take folks out windows this way. Some places they're getting them out with ladders from the second story, but there just aren't enough to go round."

He rowed off toward De Graw's up the street, and Dirck had a chance to inquire about the situation at the Queen.

"Snug and dry so far, Tinker," Mr. Sylvester assured him, "but the lower end of Albany's pretty well awash. Antje is guarding the front door with a battalion of mops."

Dirck chuckled. "And how about Mr. Farquhar, sir?" he asked curiously. "Has he gone out to help?"

Mr. Sylvester threw back his head and laughed. "Well, he had his scarf on all ready to partner me; then he remembered he'd left his coat upstairs. Last time I saw him he was rushing off to get it. Guess he must have been delayed a mite; he hasn't come back yet."

He rowed alongside a large gray house.

"Here's your loose shutter, Tinker. I think this must be De Graw's."

"It is, sir," Dirck nodded. "If you'll steady us, I'll try to see what's wrong."

Fortunately the window was close to water level and he could reach it standing up.

"Wonder how they overlooked the bar on a shutter right in front?" he muttered. "They must have left in a tearing hurry last night." He tested the latch carefully, but it refused to hold. "I'm afraid I'll have to tie this one, Mr.

Sylvester. It won't be tight enough to do much good if the water comes up, but at least it'll stay closed."

Looping a length of string from his pocket through the shutter hardware and the catch in the sill, he pulled it tight before he tied it off. He'd done the best he could, but he kept looking back uneasily as they rowed away.

"That window's a regular invitation to looters, sir. Do you think there'll be many around?"

"Not many successful ones, Tinker, if Fitten and Sturdevandt can help it. They were planning double patrols to work in relays, last I heard. Catching a few looters at work might discourage the rest for a while."

A shout from behind slowed Mr. Sylvester's stroke. The Van Arsdalen dory was bearing down on them as fast as the lockkeeper could send it through the water.

"Trouble over on Liberty Street," he called. "Fitten sent word to get over there."

"Right on your heels," Mr. Sylvester yelled back, but keeping up with Jacobus Van Arsdalen's oars was more than he'd reckoned on. The lockkeeper's boat forged so rapidly ahead that the engineer felt like a mud turtle. When he caught Dirck's eye, he smiled ruefully.

"Guess I'm a landlubber, Tinker. If you can row like your father, I'll swop seats any time you say."

"I'm no match for him either, sir," Dirck admitted promptly. "Maddy nearly is though. She's small, and maybe she'll never be quite that fast, but she rows circles around him every other way. You'd think a boat was a dog the way she teaches it tricks." He frowned thoughtfully. "Sometimes it seems an awful waste she's a girl."

Mr. Sylvester's eyes twinkled. "I don't think I'd go that far," he drawled. "My wife claims everything a girl learns comes in handy once in her life. Take egg throwing, for example; at first thought you wouldn't expect that to be especially useful, now would you?" He looked over at Dirck and grinned. "Anyway, maybe she'll marry a sailor."

For some reason, the idea of Maddy's marrying anybody gave him a jolt. Dirck examined it silently. The possibility had never crossed his mind before, and now that it had, he didn't think much of it. Some scrubbed-up, calf-eyed Dutchman mooning around the Brandt house would knock all the sense out of Maddy's head in no time. He scowled the rest of the way down to Liberty Street.

Ahead of them, halfway up the street, they saw Mr. Van Arsdalen hitch his dory to a stoop railing and dash hastily into the Van Iderstine house, Mr. Brandt so close beside him that they seemed to move as one man. Two other boats were tied alongside the front door, and four more on their way changed their course now to maintain a steady patrol around the back and sides.

"The first of the looters, I guess, Tinker." Mr. Sylvester put on a burst of speed that brought their boat alongside one of the patrols in a hurry.

"Want us inside or out?" he asked the man at the oars.

"Better hover around the front, sir; then you'll be handy if they shout. Adriense Quackenbos got suspicious when he saw a lot of household gear being loaded by strangers, so he picked up a couple of men and hustled over. It was looters all right. We were heading in ourselves till we saw

Brandt and Van Arsdalen beat us to it." He smiled drily. "With those two on hand, 'tisn't likely we'll be much needed."

As if to prove his words, the front door opened and Johann Brandt poked his head out. His face was slightly flushed, and his jacket sat askew; otherwise he looked as placid as a millpond.

"Ah, there you are, Dirck," he called cheerfully. "Some friends of yours inside, my lad. Your father wants a hand with them. Stand by for passengers, will you, gentlemen?"

Mystified, the boy climbed up on the stoop and ran inside while the patrol crews, hearing voices, gathered outside and waited expectantly. It was Mr. Sylvester, though, who recognized the first prisoner escorted out the door by Dirck Van Arsdalen.

"By George," he muttered, staring in astonishment, "the crew of the *Alligator* again. What a nestful of rotten eggs that barge has aboard her."

He shoved the dory hastily alongside so Dirck could seat his prisoner in the stern. Guarded against a sudden break-away by the ring of patrols, the man submitted sullenly to having his hands and feet tied. Dirck had had a stomach-ful of *Alligator* tricks, and he was taking no chances. Any-one taking these ropes off was going to have to cut them. He got to his feet and looked the prisoner over.

"There's seven feet nine inches of water standing down Burnet Street," he said warningly. "Make a jump for it, hog-tied this way if you want to, but it won't be smart."

Stepping into the bow, he took his seat, and Mr. Sylves-ter pulled along to let the other boats load in the last five looters. Then the little flotilla moved off toward Sturdevandt's shipyards.

"Van Iderstine rowed some people down to the Queen," Adriense Quackenbos called after them. "Send him along to get this door locked properly. I'll stay till he comes."

Mr. Van Arsdalen nodded. "We'll tend to it as soon as we get these off our hands." He looked contemptuously at the looters and dipped his oars in his mile-eating, rhythmic stroke.

Town Marshall Fitten received the consignment of looters with grim satisfaction. Fortunately the jail was beyond the flooded area, and the watch had no difficulty housing their prisoners securely.

"If we catch other looters as promptly, their game won't be worth the risk," the marshall told his volunteers, "so let's look lively. Looe has the patrol timetables. Get your hours and block assignments now. Night patrols finish up and do your sleeping this afternoon. Report direct to your block assignments; don't waste time coming here. In case you need help, headquarters patrol boats will row out on rounds every hour. One thing more: I'll repeat all this as patrols come in from duty, so let each team get its own timetable. Clear?"

"Couldn't be clearer." Opinion was unanimous. Anxious to see what they had drawn, the men clustered around Looe Sturdevandt's trestle to receive their assignments, poking good-natured fun at those who drew the longest blocks and the early morning hours.

At their own request, Johann Brandt was teamed with Jacobus Van Arsdalen, and Dirck with Mr. Sylvester, who

had lacked a partner since Mr. Farquhar defaulted. The engineer planned to snatch his afternoon sleep with the others at the lockkeeper's house and his meals with them at Brandts's.

"Tinker and I will try to catch Van Iderstine at the Queen," he volunteered, "but we'll see you around noontime at the Brandts's."

He shoved off and sprang into the stern of the dory, glad enough to let Dirck spell him at the oars. In spite of their sailcloth jackets, they were both soaked to the skin. They'd better take enough time out to pick up a couple of dry ones from his room and cajole a cup of hot soup from Antje, the engineer thought.

The rain seemed to be lessening at last. He took a look at the sky. No question about it now: the clouds were definitely breaking. Across the river, in the east, he even saw a faint patch of blue.

"Blue sky, Tinker," he called jubilantly. "Maybe tonight we'll see a star again."

Dirck looked up excitedly. "Enough blue sky to patch a Dutchman's breeches, Mr. Sylvester. That means clearing for sure. Good thing about the Raritan; she goes down as fast as she rises, given half a chance. Once the rain lets up, folks can start mopping up in two or three days. It'll seem mighty good to stay dry again, sir."

Rowing out of Burnet Street, he shipped his oars and drifted around to see what kind of a landing he could make at the Queen. Albany was awash all right; water pouring down Burnet Street and over the canal bank by the Toll Bridge had turned it into a lake that fed steadily back along Water Street beside the inn's backdoor. Yet, in spite of that, the Indian Queen must still be dry. The boy stared in amazement. Water gurgled within a foot of the front door, but thanks to the lower slope of Water Street, it never came any closer. Why, with luck, now the rain was letting up, Mr. Barckaloe would just have to pump out the cellar.

Dirck hitched the dory to a front shutter, and the pair of them scrambled out. They met Wilhelm Van Iderstine just inside the door. Rumor had already reported the looting at his house, and he was hurrying back to Liberty Street. Relieved to learn that Adriense Quackenbos still mounted guard, he rowed off in a more cheerful frame of mind.

"I'll nail up the doors and windows if I have to," he told Mr. Sylvester. "Van Iderstines' will be one house the patrols can stop worrying about when I get through with it this time."

The innkeeper and Mrs. Molenaer welcomed the latest comers heartily. The Queen, they reported, was crowded with refugees. Trina and Katje had piled feather beds in rows on the floors until bedrooms looked like barracks. Mrs. Molenaer brought them each a bowl of soup while she plied them with questions. Rumors and oddments of news trickled in with every new arrival, and the inn staff was anxious for less garbled accounts. Mr. Sylvester sketched the situation baldly; it was bad enough in reality without the grisly details rumor had conjured up.

He smiled over at Dirck. "Come along, Tinker. Dry jackets for us both up in my room; then we'd better be getting off. Which reminds me: I won't be back tonight, Mrs. Molenaer, so use my quarters if you need them."

"Thank you, sir," Antje said, as they started to tramp up the stairs. "We may come to that yet. I'd feel freer, though, if you gather up your papers and leave them with Staats."

Mr. Sylvester agreed at once. "I'll tend to it as we come down," he assured her.

Then he and Dirck were out of sight around the curve in the stairs. It felt good to pull off their wet jackets and get into the dry things Mr. Sylvester rooted out of his clothes press. Dirck looked at their sopping coats with distaste.

"I'd better take these down to the scullery, sir," he suggested. "Trina will have a fit if she finds water dripping all over this tidy floor. I'll meet you at the front door in just a second."

The engineer, busy gathering his papers and stuffing them in folders, nodded silently, and Dirck started down the corridor toward the back stairs. He was close beside the Coejemanns's door when the screams began, a woman's voice rising and wailing in hysterical crescendo. For a second the boy was too startled to move; then he turned and beat on the door with his fist.

"Mrs. Coejemann! Mrs. Coejemann!" he called frantically.

Those screams were enough to drive you crazy. Dimly, he was aware of doors banging and feet pounding up the stairs; then, with relief, of Mr. Sylvester running down the hall.

"Get that door open, Tinker," the engineer ordered as he rushed up.

"It's locked or stuck somehow. I've tried." Dirck's face was frightened. "Shall we try to break it down?"

At Mr. Sylvester's nod, they threw themselves heavily against it. Something gave a little; they could feel a tug and pull.

"Hooked probably," Guy Sylvester grunted. "Try it again, Tinker."

This time the door opened an inch, but the screw eye still held stubbornly in the heavy oak frame. Inside the room it was suddenly and terrifyingly silent. Grimly Dirck and Mr. Sylvester prepared to try once more. Panting from his headlong rush up the stairs, Staats Barckaloe added his bulky shoulders to their charge. They could hear wood splintering; then the fastening tore loose and flung them in a crazy stumble through the doorway. Dirck was on his knees by Mrs. Coejemann's crumpled figure before either of the older men had recovered his balance.

"Just fainted, I think, sir," he said, answering the engineer's question. "I don't think she's hurt any, unless maybe she bumped her head when she fell."

Catching sight of Trina's face in the crowd around the door, Mr. Barckaloe set her searching for smelling salts among the bottles on the bureau while they lifted Mrs. Coejemann onto the bed and ordered the onlookers off. The young woman's eyelids were already fluttering, and a whiff of the salts Trina waved to and fro under her nose soon had her staring wonderingly at the anxious faces bent over her. Then memory came flooding back, and she burst into tears.

Mr. Barckaloe patted her shoulder gently. "Try to stop crying, ma'am, and tell us what happened," he urged. "Did something frighten you?"

Sobbing wildly, Mrs. Coejemann shook her head. "My necklace," she gasped. "My diamond necklace; it's gone."

The men looked at each other in consternation. "Are you sure, Mrs. Coejemann?" Guy Sylvester's steady voice quieted her for a moment. "When did you see it last? Try to think for a minute."

But even half hysterical as she was, Mrs. Coejemann stuck to her story. She'd worn the necklace the night before and put it away in its own case when she went to bed. For safety's sake she'd meant to wear it at breakfast; then in the excitement of the flood she'd forgotten. She rocked back and forth in grief and despair. It was a relief to them all when her husband returned shortly from patrol duty and took her in charge. With his help, they turned out the drawers in the dressers, searched through pockets in clothing, combed every inch of the room. There was no longer a question in anyone's mind.

Once convinced that the diamonds had disappeared, Mr. Barckaloe set to work with an efficiency that belied his usual easygoing ways. The Queen's guests were assembled in the common room and the situation explained. Mr. Farquhar, fluttering genteelly in his concern for the Coejemanns, immediately demanded a search of them all and began turning his own pockets out. To the majority, his suggestion seemed eminently sensible, and they agreed to it at once as the likeliest way to remove suspicion from themselves. They even nominated the searchers unanimously: Mrs. Molenaer for the women and the innkeeper for the men.

By the time Dirck and Mr. Sylvester left, Jan, the stable boy, had returned with two of the city watch, and the inn, as well as its guests, was being given a painstaking overhauling. It seemed to Dirck as he rowed down toward the river that nothing hidden in the inn could long elude a search like this one. If the necklace didn't turn up now, it simply couldn't be in the Queen at all.

CHAPTER SIXTEEN

Prowler in the Night

DOWN BY THE Toll Bridge Dirck let the dory
drift a moment. The rain was reluctantly petering out into
a drizzle, and he could get a fairly clear view upriver. On
the farther shore, where the land lay low and swampy,
trees seemed to be growing fantastically in water up to
their topmost branches. All the gentle winding curves of
river bank and towpath that gave the Raritan its quiet,
everyday charm had vanished utterly. Before him roared
a raging, charging monster of water that scoured everything out of its path.

All of a sudden, he was bone-weary. Flood or no flood,
he wanted only to get some dinner and fall into bed and
sleep. Catching Mr. Sylvester yawning openly, he dipped
his oars again for the half-mile stretch down to Brandts's.
He didn't pay much attention to the *Alligator* riding high
at her moorings when they started to pass until Mr. Sylvester called to him. The engineer might look half asleep, but
his quick eye had noticed something amiss.

"Snubbing rope parted, I think, Tinker." He pointed.
"Look up there at the bow."

Dirck hove to alongside. Sure enough, the *Alligator* rode

free of one cable, and with all the force of the heavy current straining her stern hitch, she might go adrift any time.

"Just grab ahold of her, sir, for a minute," he said. "Maybe I can find another snubbing or splice this one."

Dropping quickly over the *Alligator's* bow, he examined the frayed rope and shook his head.

"There's an extra length of cable coiled at the stern hitch," he called to the engineer. "I'll cut a piece from that."

In no mood to waste time skirting the coal, he started straight across it, lurching awkwardly as it slipped under his feet. Halfway he lost his balance completely on a small avalanche and slid to the stern in a heap. Grimy and disgusted, he popped into sight again to set to work on the rope with his knife.

Holding the bobbing dory beside the barge with a firm grip, the engineer blinked his eyes sleepily and waited for Dirck to finish the job and come back aboard. He so nearly dropped off that his mind hardly registered the sound of Dirck's feet pounding along the *Alligator's* deck, but he caught the excitement in the boy's voice fast enough.

"Better come over yourself, sir. There's something here you'll want to see." As he spoke, he caught up the dory's painter and made her fast to the big barge. "Back there where I slid toward the stern, Mr. Sylvester," he said.

With the boy at his heels, Mr. Sylvester circled round for a look. Then he whistled sharply. Dirck's feet had disturbed a cache of stolen goods wrapped in a cloth and concealed in the coal. Leaning over, the engineer picked up a couple of silver spoons and a porringer.

"Recognize any of this stuff, Tinker?" he asked.

Dirck shook his head. "No, sir," he said regretfully, "but it might be Van Iderstines' silver, I suppose. They had a lot I've heard. Maybe one boatload got back here before Mr. Quackenbos spotted the looters this morning. Makes you laugh to remember Mr. Sturdevandt's speech when they launched the *Alligator*, sir; a lot of 'honest service' she's given so far!"

Mr. Sylvester shrugged. "We'd best gather it up and leave it with Marshall Fitten as we row by. Stow all you can in your pockets, Tinker; no use making an extra trip to the dory."

Methodically they began loading themselves: spoons, forks, knives, three porringers, a silver teapot and a silver pitcher, two cameos, a gold link necklace, several brace-lets, and a curiously chased, heavy gold ring. Dirck poked energetically around in the coal.

"That's the lot, I guess, sir."

He started to straighten up; then swooped down again suddenly, his hand groping for something still partially concealed at one side. A quick pull and he was up again, bewilderment all over his face as he stared at the old clock from the wall of the Indian Queen. Stealing silverware you could make sense of, stealing an empty clock case was just plain crazy, and he never had got the works back in it. Looking at the stains and scratches on the beautiful old mahogany, Dirck began to get mad.

"This is the Queen's clock, Mr. Sylvester," he said indignantly, "the one I've been working on. Why anyone would take that beats the Dutch. Look at the mess it's in, sir! Do we have to turn this over to Marshall Fitten, too, or can I keep it to fix? I could tell Mr. Barckaloe I have it, and Maddy'd keep it at her house till ours is dry again."

"Go ahead and hang onto it, Tinker." Guy Sylvester advised. He picked it up curiously and opened it. "It's empty all right. Jove, what a wreck; even the inside is stained. Personally I'd toss it away and get another, but I'm not Staats Barckaloe. If you can make that thing look respectable again, young fellow, you're wasting your talents as the Queen's handyman."

He handed it back with a grimace of distaste, and Dirck carried it over to the dory along with the rest of the things they'd gathered up.

When they reached Sturdevandt's, Marshall Fitten listened to their tale with an angry frown.

"I'll clap every last one of that crew I can get my hands on into jail till this is over," he growled. "Then maybe we'll have some peace around here. There's been nothing but brawling and trouble since Giles signed them on."

He itemized the pieces of jewelry and silverware and sent them on to the jail for safekeeping as soon as Mr. Sylvester signed the list. It was all right with him if Dirck kept Staats Barckaloe's clock.

"And mind," he called after them as they started off once more for Brandts's, "collar any one of those pirates you lay eyes on and turn him over to the watch."

Safely out of sight, Guy Sylvester looked over at Dirck and grinned. "With six of them under lock and key, the rest would be pretty stupid not to lie low for a spell. I doubt if Marshall Fitten overcrowds his jail with our friends from the *Alligator* tonight."

He stretched his legs wearily. "By George, I'm tired and hungry, Tinker. How about you?"

"Rowing in my sleep, sir," Dirck answered, "but Brandts's isn't far ahead."

He pulled steadily at the oars, sweeping the dory along as fast as he could in the turbulent water. The sun beginning to break through the clouds seemed only to high-light the desolation around them. He hated to think of the mud and rubbish that would be left behind when the river went down. As they passed his own house, as isolated as a lighthouse on a bit of rock offshore, he had a queer lost feeling.

After that, it was pleasant just to row up to the Brandts's back stoop, still safe above water level, and hear cheerful voices and the rattle of pans in the kitchen. His father and Mr. Brandt had got there first; he found their dory already tied up. Quickly he made Mr. Sylvester's fast and tramped after the engineer into the house to a hearty welcome. Hanging their damp jackets on wooden pegs near the stove, the pair washed up and joined the others at the big round table by the window overlooking the road.

"We saw you coming," Maddy told them, "and kept your dinner piping hot." She filled their plates and poured out tumblers full of milk while she chattered. "Father's told us all about rescuing Mrs. Vredenburg and catching the looters. Oh, Dirck, I wish I had been along; it must have been exciting wading through houses trying to get people out."

Mrs. Brandt looked reprovingly at her daughter. "Hush, Maddy. Mr. Sylvester's not used to such unladylike ways."

She turned apologetically to the engineer, but his eyes were twinkling.

"I find Miss Maddy delightful just as she is, Mrs. Brandt, and I don't blame her a bit for not liking to miss all the excitement. But wait till she hears what happened at the Queen and what Tinker found in the coal!"

He paused provokingly and took a drink of milk while everyone eyed him expectantly.

"It's really Tinker's story anyway," Mr. Sylvester continued at last. "Maybe he'd better tell it."

But Dirck shook his head. "I'm too sleepy to get it straight." He stifled a yawn. "Right now I'd have the screams aboard the *Alligator* and the coal down at the Queen."

Guy Sylvester laughed. "I'm not much better myself, so I'll make it short. Then you ladies can solve the mystery for us while we get some sleep."

Briefly he recounted the events at the Queen and Dirck's discovery of the loot in the *Alligator*. "Whether they finally found that necklace at the Queen, we don't know, of course, but I'm willing to wager they didn't. Perhaps the thief that got Mr. Ten Eyck's rubies isn't so far away as some folks thought."

Amid the torrent of exclamations and questions, Dirck remembered the clock and ran out to the dory to fetch it.

"This is the queerest thing of all," he said, showing them the battered mahogany case. "I found it in the coal with the other stuff. If it's all right with you, Mrs. Brandt,

I'd like Maddy to put it upstairs where it'll stay dry till I can work on it. Mr. Barckaloe sets great store by that clock."

"Of course it's all right, Dirck. Maddy can tuck it up on the beam by her window. It'll be safe enough there, though I must say you've got your work cut out for you if that thing's to be fit to look at again."

She smiled hospitably at them all. "You men had better turn in upstairs and get some sleep. It's no trouble," she insisted when they protested they were going down to Van Arsdalens's. "Mr. Brandt tells us you're all on patrol tonight. We've made up your beds, and we'll call you in time for a late supper. There's not a mite of sense doing any more rowing than you have to."

Maddy, running ahead to show the visitors where to sleep, watched Dirck yawn and took the clock case out of his hands in a hurry.

"I'll put it away before you swallow it," she said, laughing at him.

Dirck grinned sleepily, rubbing his eyes. "I might at that. Now scat before one of your talkative fits ruins my beauty sleep."

Maddy made a face at him and closed the door quietly behind her. Then she set the clock case away on a beam by her own window and ran downstairs.

"I guess they were all asleep before I reached the foot of the stairs," she said. "It's one o'clock now, Mother." She glanced over at the clock ticking pleasantly away on a shelf near the back door. "If they have to be back on patrol again by nine, what time should we wake them?"

166

"Quarter to eight's soon enough," Mrs. Brandt answered. "Supper'll be ready, and they don't have to go very far, any of them. Dirck and Mr. Sylvester are patrolling right around here."

The women speculated in low voices on the theft at the Queen as they worked. Over in the corner, Maddy rolled out the dough she'd set in the morning and spread it with dried apples, butter, and sugar for coffee cake. Her fingers went through the motions mechanically from long practice, but her mind kept darting off, pouncing on ideas like a cat on a mouse, only none of them seemed to explain these happenings any better. She set the coffee cakes aside to rise again and began dicing vegetables for soup.

Maybe she should feel sorrier about Mr. Ten Eyck's rubies and Mrs. Coejemann's diamonds than anything else, but if Pieter hadn't been sick and Dirck could go to Rutgers, she wouldn't care about another thing and she knew it. Dirck didn't say a word about engineering any more. He smiled and talked, but his eyes never laughed at all. She blinked back tears and sniffed angrily. What was losing a handful of old diamonds compared to having your whole life spoiled that way!

Too restless to join her mother and Mrs. Van Arsdalen when they sat down to sew, she climbed into the dory and worked off some of her pent-up emotion in a long hard row.

She'd been all the way down to Albany Street when she finally got home and ran into the kitchen to do her share toward supper. Mrs. Van Arsdalen, stirring soup at the stove, gave her a quick smile. She had caught a glimpse of the fleeting tears earlier and guessed their cause.

Maddy's expressive face was a lot easier for Margaretta Van Arsdalen to read than Pastor Howe's printed sermons, and since Pieter's illness, the girl's eyes hadn't danced with their usual mischief. But now her small chin with its deep cleft was lifted resolutely; apparently she'd tossed her discouragement into the flood waters and was ready to give battle again. It would be fun to have a daughter like Maddy, Mrs. Van Arsdalen thought; she caught herself envying Wilhelmina Brandt in a most unchristian fashion.

By half past seven Maddy's healthy Dutch appetite had grown to such proportions that she practically purred at the sight of her own coffee cakes coming hot and luscious from the oven. Why didn't fashionable people starve to death waiting for late supper every night? As soon as the clock said quarter to eight, she darted up the stairs without any urging. Mrs. Van Arsdalen laughed outright.

"I feel the same way myself. If those men are slow coming downstairs, Wilhelmina Brandt, I warn you I'll probably eat bowl and all when you serve that soup!"

"Father says to start serving, Mother," Maddy called hopefully as she returned. "They'll be here in no time at all."

Humming contentedly, she filled soup bowls and sliced coffee cake while her mother set cheese and steaming pots of hot chocolate on the table. Relaxed and rested, the men brought along appetites to match Maddy's. Night patrol wasn't half bad, they agreed, when it included a supper like this one, and they were quite willing to carry along packets of coffee cake and cheese when they left.

"We'll not be home before daylight," Johann Brandt told his wife at the door, "so forget about us and get some sleep. It's been a long day for all of you."

Standing on the back stoop, the women watched the dories fade into the darkness. The storm had finally broken the backbone of the long-drawn heat spell, and it was good just to breathe comfortably once more. Overhead the stars were shining at last.

It's just like having stars grow in your garden, Maddy thought, as she watched their reflections bobbing merrily in the water that lapped around the stone foundation of the house.

The muffled splash of oars and the flickering lantern of a patrol boat down Burnet Street made her feel comfortably secure. She hated to go in, even to help finish the dishes, but she could hardly keep her eyes open much longer. Her mother and Mrs. Van Arsdalen were no better off. They were having a hard time not to yawn as they tidied up, and no one was sorry to blow out the lamps and creep wearily into bed.

To Maddy's sleep-befuddled mind, it seemed queer to open her eyes and stare into darkness; generally it was high time to get up when she woke. She lay contentedly still, halfway between sleeping and waking. Vaguely, as though in a dream, her ear registered a sound, a quiet, stealthy footfall, and her lips curved in a sleepy smile: what funny things dreams were. Then suddenly every sense was alert. This wasn't any dream. That footstep was real; that's what had waked her.

She wanted to jump out of bed and run, to put distance

between herself and that terrifying footstep in the dark, but she didn't dare stir. Tense and motionless, she listened desperately for the next footstep. If she could only once locate those sounds, if she could only be sure the prowler wasn't in her path to the door, she might risk running. There it was again, the same soft pad of feet, now here, now there.

Strange that a looter should pick their house when so many others were empty. But, of course, he thought it was; they'd gone to bed early; there hadn't been any light. Her wits sharpened by fear, she tried to think of some way to get help. If she could make Dirck and Mr. Sylvester hear her, she'd scream for help. With fierce intensity, she began to listen for the splash of oars.

Lie still! Don't move! Over and over her mind whispered the same instructions to her frayed nerves.

Was that the patrol boat, that quiet thud against the house? She strained her ears for some way to be sure. Yes! Now she could hear Dirck's carefully lowered voice. Lifting her head to scream, Maddy forgot the need for caution until a flying figure catapulted across the room and jerked at her hair, wrenching her head back roughly.

Maddy's fear evaporated in sheer rage. Closing her teeth on the arm clamped over her face, she bit as hard as she could and hung on. Smothering a cry, the prowler momentarily released his gagging hold. That was all Maddy needed. Slippery as a fighting trout, she twisted her head aside.

"Dirck! Dirck! Help!" Her voice rang frantically through the blackness.

Almost at once she heard the bump of the dory under her back window and the pound of Dirck's feet running through the kitchen toward the stairs, then the footsteps of the engineer following him. The man beside her bed heard them, too. With a muttered oath, he fled for the far window and swung out just as Dirck banged into the room. For an instant, his hands, clinging to the sill, shone clear and white in the light of the boy's lantern; then they dropped from sight. Darting to the window, Dirck leaned hurriedly out.

"Too late," he growled to the engineer coming up beside him. "He had a dory back of the lilac bushes down there. He could find a dozen hiding places before we could even shove off after him. But if he hurt Maddy," the boy's voice was grim, "I'll find him if it takes the rest of my life."

He was hurrying back to the bed while he was talking. Mrs. Brandt, wakened by Maddy's outcry, already had her arms around her daughter, the girl's face buried on her shoulder. Beside them, Mrs. Van Arsdalen clutched a bedpost, her face white.

"Is she all right, Mother?" Dirck demanded huskily. "Did he hurt her?"

Mrs. Van Arsdalen shook her head uncertainly. "I don't know, son. I think she's more frightened than anything else, but her face looked bruised."

The boy's fists clenched and unclenched at his side. No wonder Mr. Court had thought his skull was empty when it took a thing like this to make him realize how he felt about Maddy. He reached across and put his hand over the girl's clinging to her mother's shoulder.

"Let's look at you, young'un," he coaxed. "I'll have to know just how much to muss up that man's face for you."

Maddy laughed a little as she raised her head. "My face is just sore, that's all." She touched her bruised lips and cheek. "Oh, Dirck, I was so scared, and I thought you and Mr. Sylvester would never come. I kept listening and listening, and then when I heard you, he tried to keep me from yelling by pulling my hair and putting his arm over my mouth."

Her eyes glinted with indignation; then she looked startled. "I guess I hurt him a lot more than he hurt me," she said slowly. "I bit him good and hard. That's why he let go."

Mr. Sylvester chuckled aloud. "He's already a marked man, Tinker; you can stop worrying about mussing him up. We might have guessed Miss Maddy would give a good account of herself. Now come along and let Mrs. Brandt fix up her daughter's face so they can get some sleep."

Reluctantly Dirck turned away; he was still seething with rage over Maddy's experience.

"Tinker will stay in the house the rest of the night, Mrs. Brandt," the engineer called from the doorway. "Just shout if you want him. He'll be downstairs."

Mrs. Brandt looked relieved. "We'll feel safer with you here, Dirck," she admitted. "Good night, and thank you both for coming to Maddy's aid."

Downstairs Dirck established himself in the kitchen as Mr. Sylvester prepared to leave.

"Get some sleep, Tinker," he advised. "I'll come back

for you if I run into any trouble, and Mrs. Brandt will call if she needs help. Best snatch a cat nap while you can."

Dirck nodded and flapped his hand at Mr. Sylvester in farewell. Stretching his long legs out ahead of him, he lay back in a chair near the window and tried to think of some way to identify the prowler who had invaded Maddy's room. If only there had been a moon to show them his size or high-light some feature. Finding out who it was seemed utterly hopeless, and yet he had a disquieting notion that he had overlooked some clue that might help. All he'd seen though, even for a moment in the light of his lantern, was the man's hands.

He jerked upright. That was it; that was what had been troubling him: those hands clinging momentarily to the window ledge in Maddy's room. Completely taken aback by the suspicion that had seized his mind, he closed his eyes and tried to visualize the scene exactly. Maybe his idea wouldn't make sense to anybody else; maybe people would think he had gone completely crazy. Just the same he knew now where he had seen those hands before!

CHAPTER SEVENTEEN

Heinie

ONCE WHILE IT was still dark, Dirck woke in alarm at the sound of footsteps on the back stoop, but it was only Mr. Sylvester returning from patrol. Stretching himself out on the settle in the corner, the engineer dropped off to sleep, and Dirck dozed peacefully again. Mrs. Brandt's firm tread in the room over the kitchen finally roused him to full consciousness. Sunrise was long past. He glanced over at the settle, but Mr. Sylvester still slept heavily, his head pillowed on his folded jacket.

Quietly Dirck slipped off his chair and tiptoed out to the stoop. Dragonflies streaked over the sunlit water washing against the house, and a pair of jays squawked in the big elm down by the barn. Lazily rubbing the sleep out of his eyes, the boy looked for his father and Mr. Brandt, but not a patrol boat was in sight.

Ambling across to the wash shed at one end of the stoop, he proceeded to strip and pump a stream of icy water over his head and shoulders. That stirred him up all right. He pummeled himself dry and ran back to the kitchen. His appetite was suddenly wide awake and demanding attention. Maybe he'd better get Mr. Sylvester up after all so

Mrs. Brandt could cook breakfast. At Dirck's prodding, the engineer opened one eye and yawned prodigiously.

"What's the idea of waking a man in the middle of the night?" he grumbled good-naturedly, but he got to his feet in a hurry and disappeared in the direction of the wash shed when he heard Mrs. Brandt heading downstairs.

Dirck was energetically thumping the cushions on the chair and the settle they had slept on when she entered the room.

"Is Maddy all right?" he asked at once. Then he remembered his manners and flushed. "I mean good morning, Mrs. Brandt," he emended hastily.

She smiled. "Good morning, Dirck. Maddy's bemoaning a swollen lip, but she'll be down in a moment. I'm grateful she hasn't anything more than a bruise or two. Do you suppose that man was another looter from the *Alligator's* crew? I'll feel a lot more comfortable when all those men are safely locked up."

Dirck listened sympathetically, but he didn't say much. He'd feel better himself if Marshall Fitten could clap the entire *Alligator* crew into jail; still, he didn't think any of them had been prowling around Maddy's room last night. If his eyes weren't playing tricks on him, that hadn't been any bargeman. As soon as he got a chance, he'd get Mr. Sylvester's advice. Until then he'd have to keep it to himself. You couldn't go around accusing an apparently respectable man because you thought you recognized his hands by lantern light.

Though no matter what anyone says, he insisted stubbornly to himself, I did recognize them.

He cornered Maddy as soon as she came down and went over the night's experiences with her while his mother and Mrs. Brandt were getting breakfast on the table. The girl eyed him shrewdly.

"You think you know who it was, don't you, Dirck?" she said in a low voice. "I wish I could help you. I've tried and tried, but I can't even remember the sound of his voice when he swore."

She frowned thoughtfully; then all of a sudden she seized Dirck's arm, her voice an excited undertone. "I bit him hard enough to make him let go. It was his right arm, Dirck. It must have been because he was on the right side of my bed when he grabbed me. If you find marks on the right forearm of the man you suspect, you can be sure he's the prowler; I know you can!"

"That would be proof enough for anyone I guess, Maddy. We all know you bit him. The only trouble," the boy sounded disgusted, "is getting a chance to see his arm. I can't go running up to him and push up his sleeve." He glanced over at the engineer just coming back to sit down at the breakfast table. "Maybe Mr. Sylvester can suggest something when I tell him about it, but don't you say a word now, Maddy. Promise?"

The girl nodded willingly, and they joined the others at the table in time to hear Mr. Sylvester give the two women a message from their husbands.

"They won't be back for breakfast," he told them. "I should have let you know before, but in the excitement last night it slipped my mind. Staats Barckaloe joined their patrol, and they rowed him back to the Queen. It seemed such a long trip back they thought they'd sleep there and come on home after breakfast."

"Did Mr. Barckaloe say whether they'd found Mrs. Coejemann's necklace?" Dirck asked interestedly.

The engineer nodded. "According to his account, they turned the place upside down, but they found no trace of the diamonds in the inn or on any of the guests. I'm not surprised. Whoever took that necklace was too clever to leave it very long at the Queen where the hue and cry would be hottest. To tell the truth, right now I don't believe they'd give much for their chances of finding it at all."

"I should think it would be largely good luck if they do recover it," Mrs. Brandt said soberly. "They can't search the town the way they did the Queen. I'm afraid it's gone as hopelessly as Mr. Ten Eyck's rubies."

Finally dismissing Staats Barckaloe's worries, she began to plan for the day ahead.

"Your mother wants to get fresh clothing for Pieter from your house, Dirck. Then she can take it to him this morning as soon as a boat can be spared. She'll feel better when she knows how he's getting on at Dr. Schureman's, and I think I'll go along. It's high time we saw the sights anyhow. You and Maddy can be crewmen if you will." She smiled at the boy and girl.

"Let Dirck be crew, Mother," Maddy said reluctantly. "I've still got the chickens cooped up in the barn loft. It's nice to know they're dry, but I guess they don't want to be so dry they're thirsty."

"No trick to solving that problem," Mr. Sylvester cut in.

"I'll crew the ladies, and we'll drop you and Tinker off at the barn on our way. By the time we're back, your father will be here to sign me on with him for a spell. That way you'll have a boat for your own cruise."

That plan suited everybody, and the women hustled off to their jobs around the house. Dirck wanted to tell Mr. Sylvester about his suspicions of last night's prowler, but he hated to get started and have to stop before he could finish. In the end, he was glad he hadn't tried to talk to the engineer, for his mother and Mrs. Brandt were soon ready. As he helped them into the dory and untied the painter, he could hear Maddy's flying feet on the stairs. Then she was settled in the bow, trimming ship as he hopped in and cast off.

It seemed strange to row through the barn door and over to the loft ladder. There was plenty of water in here, all right. Cooping the hens in the loft and leading the cow up the hill to Van Wagenen's had been a wise precaution. He supposed Mr. Sylvester would have to row through the front door at their house, too, and over to the stairs. If it looked the way Vredenburgs's had yesterday morning, his mother was going to be miserable at the watery mess in her tidy rooms. Clinging to the ladder with one hand, he waved at the retreating dory before he climbed nimbly after Maddy.

Chickens scattered in all directions as they lifted the trap door and stepped out into the loft, but Dirck was too amused at the outraged look Maddy turned on the littered floor to pay attention to their antics.

"Never mind, young'un," he consoled her. "I'll help you

clean up one morning right after the flood goes down."

Maddy wrinkled her nose at him. "Maybe," she said skeptically, "but I won't sit around counting on it."

She seized a broom and began to sweep vigorously, ignoring the hens' indignant protests. Dirck watched, grinning.

"That's an awful waste of energy," he remarked sagely. "You'll just have to do it all over again when you turn these chickens loose."

Maddy swept a trifle more vigorously. "There's no need to conserve my energy," she retorted. "The way you're saving yours, you'll be plenty strong enough to do my chores right along with your own all week."

Unabashed, Dirck gave a flyaway curl a reproving tweak as he gathered up the empty water pan and climbed down the ladder to fill it from the flooded barn.

"Nothing like a stream practically at your feet," he remarked when he reappeared. "That feed up here in this corner?"

At Maddy's nod, he opened the bag and scattered the grain by the handful, lazily watching the hens scurry to peck. Maddy put aside her broom and joined him for a moment; then they began a search for eggs.

"Just think where you'd lay an egg if you were a hen," Maddy advised him after he'd overlooked a couple, but Dirck rejected the idea with scorn.

"Not even for scrambled eggs and sausage will I go around trying to act like a hen," he told her indignantly. "If that's what you do everyday, it's no wonder you're scatterbrained half the time."

He hunted in silence for a minute and triumphantly added a half dozen more to Maddy's basket. "Bet I find more than you do anyway," he was beginning, when he broke off to listen. "Boat coming, Maddy; hear it? Mr. Sylvester wouldn't be back yet, so I guess it's Father and Mr. Brandt."

He walked over to the loft window for a look, and the girl, a step or two behind him, heard him gasp. Signaling for silence, he pulled her forward and pointed toward the Brandts's stoop where someone with his back to them was tying a rowboat to the railing. Stopping for just a second to glance over his shoulder, the man climbed quickly out and ran for the kitchen door. Maddy stared in bewilderment.

"Who is it, Dirck?" she whispered. "Did you see his face?"

The boy nodded angrily. "It's Heinie again, the man you threw the egg at, and he has no business in your house. You wait here, Maddy; I'm going after him."

Dirck's lips were set in a thin line, and his face was hard. Watching him, Maddy was worried.

"If you go, I go," she said firmly. "Like as not, he'll try to batter your head in again, and I'm not going to be stuck up here where I can't help. It'd be different if he fought fair."

Stubborn as a tow mule, she tilted her head up at the tall boy in front of her, ready to brush any arguments aside. "What do we do, Dirck? Swim? We haven't any boat, remember."

The boy thought fast. "I'd forgotten that," he admitted.

"Look, Maddy, if I swim over and tow his boat back, will you promise to stay right here?"

Maddy nodded promptly. "That's much better than going after him into the house. He can't get away without his boat. I'll stay right here, honest."

Tense with excitement, she took a stand by the window where she could watch. Below her, she heard Dirck drop into the water and then, a moment later, saw him strike out across the yard toward the stoop. After that, she kept an anxious eye on the kitchen door. If only Mr. Sylvester would come with the boat! Suppose Heinie should catch Dirck cutting the painter of his dory. The advantage would be all on his side and he wouldn't hesitate to use it. Dirck would have to climb out of the water somehow to defend himself at all.

Maddy shivered, clutching the window sill with a grip that made her hands ache, until she saw Dirck slash the dory loose and start safely back. She could see his hands on the stern propelling the boat ahead of him. Deserting the window, she snatched up a piece of line and climbed down the ladder ready to help. As he swam the dory over, Dirck's head popped into sight, a triumphant grin on his face.

"Got her," he said laconically.

Maddy swung over the edge of the ladder, hooking the boat securely with her foot.

"Hurry up and climb out," she ordered briskly. "I'll tie her up. You go get into Father's work clothes. There are some breeches and a shirt on a peg by the hay."

She dropped lightly into the boat and began replacing

the cut painter with her line, shoving off a bit to avoid the water splashing down in the wake of Dirck's upward climb. She was just finishing when she heard the splash of oars again. Rowing hastily over to the door, she peered cautiously out, careful to keep out of sight herself. It might be her father and Mr. Van Arsdalen or Mr. Sylvester, but it could be another bargeman from the *Alligator* looking for Heinie. Her heart thudding, Maddy waited for the dory to come round the side of the house.

The sight of Mr. Sylvester gave a quick lift to her spirits. He was making straight for the barn, glancing over his shoulder for direction and rowing at a good clip. Maddy sat quietly, afraid to show herself for fear he'd call out. She was sure Heinie must have heard the oars, too. He was probably lurking somewhere in the house hoping the rowboat would go by.

The engineer looked pleased at the sight of the dory when he rowed through the door. "Your father and Mr. Van Arsdalen are back then," he said eagerly, but Maddy shook her head and signaled hastily for a lower voice. Quickly she led the way to the ladder where Dirck, perched on a rung, waited impatiently to tell their story. The boy made it as brief as he could, spilling the words out in a rush.

"Heinie's mean, Mr. Sylvester—nasty mean, Henrik Coenraad says," Dirck concluded. "Whatever he's after, he's working out his spite damaging things in the Brandt house because Maddy hit him with that egg. When I was cutting the dory loose, I could hear him throwing things around upstairs."

But the engineer shook his head. "There's something

182

queer going on, Tinker. I came back hoping your father was around by now. Someone's paid a visit to your house, too; the second floor is a shambles; everything upside down. I sent one of my workmen over to stay with the women, so they're safe enough, and we'd better tend to this business right here quick. It looks to me as though your friend Heinie wanted something mighty bad to search two houses for it."

Loading Dirck aboard his dory, he gave Maddy crisp orders to stay at a reasonably safe distance in the rear and started rowing for the house. Astride the dory's bow as forward lookout, Dirck spotted the back door opening when they were halfway across the yard and gave terse warning. Mr. Sylvester dug in his oars for the final dash, but Heinie, desperate at the loss of his boat, plunged unhesitatingly off the stoop into the water. Dirck had one quick glimpse of something like a parcel clutched in his hand; then man and parcel sank out of sight.

The boy's mind raced. Heinie had dropped off the side closest to the wooded slopes of Johann Langveldt's bluff rising high above the Brandt property. Maybe he was as awkward a swimmer as most bargemen, but after all he couldn't have more than a couple of dozen yards to go. If he reached the woods, they'd have Old Nick's own time catching him. Dirck looked hurriedly around for Maddy; she couldn't stay safely in the rear now. Mr. Sylvester simply wasn't oarsman enough for a fast job; besides, he didn't know the terrain.

"He's started for Langveldt's bluff, Maddy. Head him off, quick!"

Taken too much by surprise to protest, the startled engineer saw Maddy streak past them, her oars flashing in a queer scudding stroke that swallowed distance whole. He bent hard to his own oars; what under the sun had possessed Tinker to send the girl ahead after a man like Heinie? Then Maddy's voice floating clearly back from the other side of the house told them she'd sighted their quarry, and the engineer redoubled his efforts.

As he rowed past the corner of the stoop, a sudden splash and a lightening of the boat jerked his head around in a hurry. Dirck was racing through the water toward the spot where Maddy's dory blocked the bargeman's progress. Guy Sylvester could hear the man snarl angrily as he tried to grab the boat rail, but Maddy was too wise to let him get a grip. Cool and wary, she played the bargeman shrewdly, her boat in constant motion, tantalizingly just beyond reach, effectively barring his escape.

Fiercely absorbed in his struggle to outwit the girl in the boat, Heinie wasn't even aware of Dirck's approach until the boy was nearly on top of him, trying to get a strangle hold on his neck. In the water the bargeman was no match for Dirck Van Arsdalen. Buoyant as cork, the boy made short work of his opponent, and Mr. Sylvester, ranging alongside, got a grip on his collar and yanked him unceremoniously into the rowboat. Maddy hastily pulled off her painter, and Dirck, clambering aboard, used it to fasten their prisoner's wrists securely.

He looked down at the bargeman in the bottom of the boat, frowning, his mind in turmoil. How did Heinie's search of the Brandt house fit in with Maddy's prowler last night? There had to be some connection; it couldn't be coincidence when two men were suddenly interested in the same place this way. But why Van Arsdalens's too? Slowly the pieces of the puzzle were beginning to fall into place; the picture wasn't all clear yet, but it would be soon.

The squarish bulge under Heinie's tightly buttoned jacket made Dirck's fingers itch. If it was what he expected, the last pieces of the puzzle would fit; but he sat quietly until they reached the stoop again and hauled Heinie into the kitchen. Dirck had a moment of dismay at the thought of Mrs. Brandt's face when she found water from their clothes pooled all over her floor. Mr. Sylvester, however, wasn't worrying about housewifely comments. Collaring the bargeman firmly, he spun the man about to face the window.

"Unbutton his jacket, Tinker," he said quietly. "Let's see what he found worth all this risk."

For one wild moment, Heinie's eyes darted around the room seeking some means of escape; then his foot caught Dirck's wrist, kicking the boy's arm away. The next moment the engineer's fist sent him sprawling. Choking back a frightened cry, Maddy sprang across to Dirck to examine the hand already beginning to swell at his side. Her quick fingers explored gently while the engineer, with no compunctions, tore two of Mrs. Brandt's dish towels in half, knotting them into rope with which he bound Heinie's ankles.

"I'm confoundedly sorry, Tinker," he said. "I should have known he'd try something. Any bones broken, Miss Maddy?"

The girl shook her head happily. "No real damage done, but if you'll hand me a piece of one of those towels, Mr. Sylvester, I'll try to keep it from swelling much more."

Ignoring Dirck's impatient protest, she bound up the wrist expertly before she turned him loose. Heinie, meanwhile, lay where he had fallen, his face sullen and morose. Now the engineer jerked him back to his feet and shoved him into a chair.

"Any more tricks out of you," he growled, "and I'll put you to sleep for a spell."

He tapped a heavy stick of wood significantly before he leaned over and pulled the man's coat open revealing the Queen's battered mahogany clock. Dirck was reaching for it almost before the others had fully grasped what it was.

"The clock again," he muttered. "I thought it would be, and this time it's going to make sense."

Putting the clock case on the kitchen table, he opened the door just as Mr. Sylvester had opened it yesterday when they found the clock in the pile of coal on the *Alligator*. Still empty. Glancing over at Heinie slumped in his chair, Dirck surprised a gleam of malicious triumph in his eyes before his face went blank again. Sure he was on the right track, the boy picked up the clock and examined it attentively, studying the scratches one by one.

"The bottom's been pried off and fastened on again," he exclaimed excitedly. He held the case out to Maddy and Mr. Sylvester. "See where their knife slipped?"

Snatching up a kitchen knife with his good left hand, Dirck inserted the blade in a fractional crack at the base of the case and pried carefully. At the same moment

Heinie galvanized into furious speech, mouthing wild threats and cursing hoarsely. But Mr. Sylvester was in no mood to listen; disgustedly he parted with a couple of pocket handkerchiefs and gagged the man effectually.

"All right, Tinker; carry on," he said.

Beckoning the others closer, Dirck slipped the loosened wood away and held the clock case up for their inspection. Inside the bottom, it was carefully packed with layers of cotton batting.

"The necklaces!" he shouted. His fingers tore the stuffing apart. "The diamond and ruby necklaces!" His hand shaking, he held both strings aloft, sparkling fire in the sunlight.

CHAPTER EIGHTEEN

Set a Thief to Catch a Thief

MR. VAN ARSDALEN and Mr. Brandt, mooring their dory at the back stoop and tramping into the kitchen, stood immobile in the doorway, utterly bewildered at the scene before them: the bargeman tied and gagged; Maddy and Mr. Sylvester both talking at once; and Dirck, wildly elated, dangling the necklaces from his fingers. Mr. Van Arsdalen recovered his wits first. Striding over to his son, he lifted the jewels from his hand, studying them hurriedly.

"The Ten Eyck rubies and the Coejemann diamonds." His voice rumbled in excitement. "How came they here, Dirck?"

But Dirck was too exuberant to be coherent, and Guy Sylvester spoke for them all. Johann Brandt's face went white as he heard the story of the prowler. He held his daughter's hand tight while the engineer retold their morning's adventures, warm in his praise of the level-headed thinking Maddy and Dirck had used.

"Apparently Heinie was hidden where he saw Tinker carry the clock case away from the *Alligator* yesterday, and when he didn't find it at your house, Van Arsdalen, he continued the search here. But one thing sure: he wasn't aboard the *John Neilson* when the rubies disappeared; he can't be the original thief."

Dirck could contain himself no longer. "But I know who the real thief is now, sir," he cried. "I recognized his hands hanging on to Maddy's window sill last night when he was hunting for the clock in her room—only, of course, I didn't know it was the clock he was after then. Heinie's just an underling, Mr. Sylvester. The 'slick crook' the revenue men are after is Mr. Farquhar down at the Queen!"

"Dirck!" His father was scandalized. "Do you realize what you're saying? Why, the man's an old friend of the Coejemanns, I hear, respectable people."

But Dirck refused to be shaken from his conviction. "I don't think he's really an old friend, Father," he maintained stoutly. "Everyone just took it for granted because he was always hanging around them, and they had to introduce him to people. Anyway I recognized his hands. I'd know them anywhere; they're different."

Mr. Van Arsdalen would have started another protest, but Mr. Sylvester gave him no chance.

"Crazy as it sounds, Tinker may have got hold of something. He doesn't usually go off half-cocked. However, proving it will be another story."

"Not proving whether he was the prowler in my room, Mr. Sylvester," Maddy broke in. "That's easy. Don't forget I bit him."

"Don't worry; he'll have the marks of Maddy's teeth on his arm all right. See if he doesn't." Dirck's tone challenged the world.

Abruptly the engineer got to his feet. "There's just one way to find that out," he said decisively. "Let's get down to the Queen before he skips town. If he's the man we want, I suspect he'd be gone now had he been able to lay his hands on the clock."

Routing Heinie out of the chair, he removed the gag and loosened the ankle straps before he propelled him to the door.

"Perhaps confronting the gentleman with the clock and this specimen may help somewhat. Here, Tinker, you can't row with that wrist; you take charge of the clock. Van Arsdalen, you're the fastest oar, so slip ahead with Tinker and explain to Fitten. If you can pick up that Federal man from my shore crew down at Sturdevandt's—he's helping Fitten—so much the better. He'll know what we ought to do. Wait for us there anyway. Brandt and I will convoy Heinie, and Miss Maddy can drop off at your house to row the women over to Dr. Schureman's when they're ready."

Johann Brandt at the oars regarded Heinie warily. "Put him in the stern," he growled. "Even tied up, he'll bear watching."

Shoving the bargeman into the dory, Guy Sylvester climbed in himself. "I'll do better than that," he promised. "I'll be in the stern beside him."

He pushed off and dropped onto the seat, quickly re-tightening the towels binding Heinie's legs. Ahead of them the lockkeeper was setting a stiff pace, and Mr. Brandt increased the speed of his own stroke, but the engineer scarcely noticed. His arm hooked securely through

Heinie's, he was trying to test Dirck's theory for himself. He wasn't convinced yet that the bargeman hadn't been working on his own, stealing from the original thief when opportunity offered.

About George Farquhar there were few facts to go on. Mr. Sylvester remembered how he had lamented the failure to discover the loss of the rubies until too late to search the steamboat passengers and how he had fluttered over the Coejemanns yesterday, demanding an immediate search of everyone at the inn. He'd protested glibly enough, but always safely after the event. Maybe they'd never know whether he was the smuggler, but if he turned out to be the Brandts's prowler, there wasn't any question about his being the thief, not with that clock case on the premises.

Only how had he known who had it? He'd stayed snug enough at the Queen, apparently. There was just one logical answer after all: he'd learned it from a confederate, from Heinie, of course. Tinker was right. Mr. Sylvester turned and stared at the bargeman.

"So you weren't the Van Arsdalens's visitor," he said quietly. "That was Gentleman George, too, but he was willing enough to let you risk your neck in a daylight raid while he kept under cover. Too bad the place wasn't as empty as you thought it was when you saw me row the ladies away. Farquhar won't be pleased, Heinie; likely he'll let you take the blame. After all, he still has the smuggled jewels, hasn't he? Why should he worry about you?"

Narrowly Guy Sylvester watched the angry glare in the

bargeman's eyes. The man was slow-witted, but his instinct for self-preservation was normal enough. Well, he'd given him something to mull over the rest of the way. The engineer began to think that they'd get to the bottom of the whole business yet. The dapper gentleman at the Queen had a smooth tongue, but it wouldn't lie him out of trouble this time if Heinie suspected he was being tossed to the wolves and lost that ugly temper of his.

Mr. Brandt turned their dory in at the Sturdevandt shipyards to find Marshall Fitten and John Hagan, the revenue officer assigned to Mr. Sylvester's shore crew, ready for them. His father had insisted that Dirck outline his own story, adding only that the engineer thought there might be something in the boy's theory and was on his way with the captured bargeman. The marshall would have been content just to lay another of the *Alligator's* crew by the heels, but he had listened as attentively as Hagan to Dirck Van Arsdalen's story. When it was told, he had quietly assigned a man to take his place and climbed into the oarsman's seat of his own dory, holding it steady for John Hagan. This was the Federal man's problem, and Marshall Fitten was at his disposal.

With Heinie under Fitten's watchful eye, Guy Sylvester stepped out and drew Hagan aside to sketch the conclusions he'd reached on the trip down Burnet Street and describe the ideas he'd planted in the bargeman's mind. Hagan nodded approvingly.

"Let's get on with it," he said urgently. "It looks as if young Van Arsdalen had solved our problem."

Stepping back into the marshall's dory, he signaled the

three boats forward, passing the engineer's comments on to Fitten as he rowed. Just before they were ready to cross into Albany Street, he halted their flotilla.

"Farquhar's room is where?" he asked Dirck.

"Second floor facing Water Street, middle room of the three down there," the boy answered promptly. "One window overlooking the river."

Hagan looked pleased. "If he's up there, we can get Heinie in before he can spot him. Marshall, that'll be up to you. If he's in the common room, tell him you want to talk confidentially somewhere; tell him you want him to test a theory about the Coejemann diamonds. Tell him anything you like, but get him up to his room if he's not there already.

"Mr. Van Arsdalen, leave your son at the kitchen door and then stay nearby. I think the fellow's too cool to make a break for it, but he's not likely to be fast enough to elude you if he does. Mr. Brandt and Mr. Sylvester stay here with Heinie until they get my signal. Young Van Arsdalen with the run of the place will tell me when the coast is clear. I'll be close to the front door. All straight?"

They nodded soberly, and the marshall's dory, with Hagan at the oars now, headed over Albany to the Indian Queen. Dirck's heart was hammering, but he never doubted his own identification of Mr. Farquhar's hands. He'd studied them too carefully, fascinated by the long tapering fingers. He'd thought them sensitive enough to be a musician's; instead they'd been sensitive enough to open Captain Frazee's safe.

His own hands were cold when he stepped through the

Queen's back door, a discreet interval after Marshall Fitten had been landed at the front. Glancing back, he saw his father slip a bit further down Water Street. The boy noted that he didn't ship his oars. The lockkeeper might still be skeptical, but he was taking no chances. Pausing only to greet Mrs. Molenaer, Dirck strode through the kitchen.

Once in the common room, however, he slowed his pace to a casual stroll, stopping to answer guests who hailed him along the way. Across the room he saw Mr. Farquhar and Marshall Fitten, in earnest conversation, start together for the stairs. The boy's eyes shone. So far Mr. Hagan's plans were working. Staats Barckaloe raised inquiring eyebrows.

"Something happened?" he asked quietly.

Leaning over the desk, the boy spoke rapidly in a low voice, and after one startled look, the innkeeper kept his face impassive. Rising calmly, he walked over to the door with Dirck, chatting casually of flood conditions in his usual hearty voice. He was laughing good-naturedly as they opened the door and stepped out on the dry wedge of sidewalk just above water level. Once outside, his tone changed abruptly.

"Get the man Heinie up the back stairs. I'll see to it there's no outcry in the kitchen."

He turned back into the Queen, and John Hagan, on watch nearby, materialized at Dirck's side. Satisfied with the innkeeper's suggestion, he rowed off, and Dirck saw Mr. Brandt's dory turning into Albany Street as he reentered the common room himself. Dropping into his customary role at the inn, he gathered up a tray full of mugs and carried it out to the kitchen. Mr. Barckaloe had evidently prepared Antje Molenaer, for she had laid down the law to her staff. Trina's frightened eyes followed the three men as they led Heinie over to the back stairs, but the rest kept up a dutiful conversational buzz. Dirck noted with complete approval that Heinie was efficiently gagged again.

The innkeeper didn't need to be told that he was most valuable at his usual post; he went reluctantly back to the common room to assemble every guest in the inn on some pretext and prevent a panic of conjecture. Dirck followed the little procession up the stairs. Halfway up, Mr. Hagan beckoned to him.

"Go along with Mr. Sylvester," he whispered. "Follow his leads and you'll know what to say. We'll have Heinie in earshot."

He trailed them to the top for a quick survey and pointed with satisfaction to the open transom over Mr. Farquhar's door down the corridor. Then he vanished, and Dirck followed Mr. Sylvester to Room 12 where the engineer thumped energetically at the door.

"Open up, Farquhar," he called. "Wait till you hear what you've missed cooped up down here all morning."

But as the door swung open and he saw Marshall Fitten, too, Mr. Sylvester apologized. "Sorry. I didn't realize you had company."

The marshall made light of their interruption. "Let's hear this news, Mr. Farquhar, shall we? I've been as cooped up at Sturdevandt's as you have at the Queen, you know."

He closed the door and looked expectantly at Mr. Sylvester and Dirck as Mr. Farquhar pulled up chairs for them and got his own pipe going.

"By George, but you must have heard this news, Fitten: how the boy here and Maddy Brandt caught a crewman from the *Alligator* red-handed with the Ten Eyck rubies and the Coejemann diamonds. We sent posthaste down to Sturdevandt's to let you know."

Marshall Fitten sprang out of the chair he'd just settled in.

"Is that the truth, Sylvester?" he demanded. He managed to look utterly dumbfounded. "I must have been on my way here before your message could reach me." Glancing over at Mr. Farquhar, he shook his head wonderingly. "Well, I guess that disposes of the little theory I came to consult you about, sir."

Marshall Fitten was playing his role of surprise conscientiously, but there was no mistaking the bombshell exploding about the ears of the dapper fashion plate who had been smoking so casually when they sat down. For a second, Mr. Farquhar's face drained white, but he rallied himself quickly.

"Forgive me if I'm bewildered, gentlemen," he exclaimed. "We'd really despaired, the Coejemanns and I, and good news on the heels of bad carries its own shock." He drew a nervous breath. "Has the rascal been identified? Has he talked?"

In spite of himself, a sharp urgency shrilled the man's voice.

Mr. Sylvester settled leisurely in his chair, crossing his legs comfortably before he answered.

"Talked?" he said disgustedly. "No, Farquhar, he's as mum as an oyster, but what good would talk do him, caught with the stuff like that? He turns out to be that fellow Heinie who tried to bash in young Van Arsdalen's head awhile back. Sort of evens old scores that you caught him, eh, Tinker?"

Dirck nodded. "I get the last laugh this time, sir, all right."

Mr. Farquhar shuddered. "An ugly brute, Tinker; I've seen him hanging around the waterfront myself and marked him down as a cutthroat best given a wide berth. The town's a safer place with him off the streets at night."

Mr. Sylvester smiled thinly. "We can echo that statement, too. Apparently he was prowling about the Brandt house last night; frightened Miss Maddy into calling for the watch, but we got there just too late. Tinker figured he wanted something mighty bad when he turned up again this morning. Strangest thing of all though was finding the necklaces in the bottom of Barckaloe's broken clock! Tinker picked it up in the *Alligator's* coal yesterday, and Heinie came chasing right after it."

Mr. Farquhar cut in on the marshall's exclamations almost at once.

"Just a moment, gentlemen," he said. "Perhaps I can help you there. Yes, I believe I can. It was yesterday morning that I saw the fellow hanging about the Queen. In fact, he stepped across the common room once to my knowledge. At the time I thought he was looking for Captain Giles, who had been in earlier, but that must have been when he got Mrs. Coejemann's diamonds and carried off the clock."

He was still smiling at his ability to be of service when an uproar began outside his door. Crazy with rage, Heinie tore loose from his captors and threw himself forward. His legs had been unbound for the walk through the inn and he moved fast, picking furiously at the knob with his roped hands. Another lunge and he was through the door, head lowered, charging into George Farquhar, toppling him backward. John Hagan's powerful arms hauled him off his victim with speedy efficiency, but it took Johann Brandt as well to hold him quiet.

Mr. Sylvester gave the man on the floor a hand up. "You don't seem overpopular with our friend Heinie, Farquhar," he drawled. "Perhaps he disagrees with your version of the Coejemann robbery."

Mr. Farquhar's face was livid. "Naturally," he snapped. "A desperate man will go to any length to save his skin."

"Suppose we hear what Heinie has to say," Hagan suggested equably. "He seems to have found his tongue all at once."

Reaching up, he untied the gag in the bargeman's mouth, and Heinie foamed into a raging tide of accusations.

"The man's mad!" Mr. Farquhar was icily disdainful when the panting rafter stopped at last for want of breath. "Fortunately there's small need for me to defend myself against such preposterous charges, but Mr. and Mrs. Coejemann can assure you I spent last evening with them.

We sat late over cards and parted close to midnight at my door.

"I'm no oarsman, Marshall; I'd founder long before I could reach Mr. Brandt's house, of whose location, as a matter of fact, I've not the faintest notion. The storm conditions since I reached New Brunswick have scarcely tempted me to explore the countryside."

He shrugged contemptuously. "My patience with this fellow is wearing thin. The sooner you rid me of him, the better."

Dirck listened, hardly crediting his own ears. The man's effrontery beggared belief. It was easy to understand why Heinie shouted and raved when a crook like this one was pushing him into jail to save his own hide. Suddenly the boy's anger reached the boiling point. Mr. Farquhar and his sneers and his lies were intolerable.

Almost of its own volition, Dirck's hand shot out, catching the man's coat by its collar and stripping it off his back. Mr. Farquhar's face lost its suave mask. His features contorted, he whirled like a cat and sprang at Dirck's throat. Then Heinie's foot, catching him between the legs, threw him off balance, and Dirck closed in fast. His shoulder pinned Mr. Farquhar against the wall; his hand ripped his shirt sleeve open.

"Take a look at his right forearm, Mr. Sylvester," he panted triumphantly.

Midway between wrist and elbow, like a neat purple tattoo, lay the double lines of Maddy's bite.

CHAPTER NINETEEN

Mop Up

THE QUEEN simmered over the week end like a pot of soup on the back of the stove. Even flooded streets couldn't keep the hordes of townsmen away. Patrols coming off duty stopped by for the latest news before they went home to catch up on sleep. Marshall Fitten and John Hagan strode in at odd moments, systematically going over George Farquhar's possessions, asking questions, tirelessly checking and rechecking their facts.

The Queen's guests had been stunned. If none of them had liked Mr. Farquhar overmuch, certainly no one had remotely connected him with the thefts. At first they were incredulous, but the bargeman Heinie, enraged by his confederate's attempt to let him shoulder all the blame, left them no room for doubt. He turned state's evidence.

According to his deposition, the pair had worked together occasionally in the past, and Farquhar had sought him out again when he first conceived the idea of using the canal as a safe means of transporting his smuggled stones. It hadn't been hard to land a berth on one of the new barges or to persuade a number of petty waterfront thieves to sign on with him. They didn't know what was up, but a shady deal wouldn't worry them any if they eventually tumbled to the smuggling game.

Knowing that Farquhar was bringing the jewels through on the *John Neilson,* Heinie had contrived to get the *Alligator's* crew drunk and hold the barge over in New Brunswick to await the transfer of the stones to his care. Then he planned to take them downriver to Perth Amboy and back to Philadelphia on the next haul. It might be slow, but they figured it was safe.

And luck had been with them in the beginning. By chance Farquhar had spotted Nicholas Ten Eyck making his purchase in the jeweler's and recognized him later as they boarded the steamboat. After that, he'd made it his business to keep an eye on the New Brunswicker until he turned a parcel over to Captain Frazee. From then on, it was only a question of opportunity, and the collision supplied that. The revenue man had persisted in nosing around below decks instead of rushing out with the rest of the passengers and crew, so Farquhar had hastily put him out of the way.

It had been plain sailing before the storm broke and tied them up in New Brunswick, but Farquhar tried to make the most of their enforced stay. Cooped up at the Queen with the Coejemann diamonds within easy reach, he had helped himself to them, too, and with the chase uncomfortably close, bundled them and the rubies into the clock case and turned them over to Heinie. Dirck Van Arsdalen's removal of the clock from the coal, however, had spelled disaster and started the sequence of events that led to their capture.

Thoroughly jolted out of their sleepy summer peace by the triple impact of smuggling, flood and theft, New Brunswickers rolled up their sleeves and went to work. By Sunday, when the last of the *Alligator's* crew had been rounded up, and the revenue officer had found the smuggled pearls hidden in a hollow tip under the ferrule of George Farquhar's cane, people began to feel that the situation was no longer out of hand.

The Raritan, comfortably back between its own banks, still looked a trifle bloated, but it was reassuringly normal to see fishermen and steamboats busy again, and to watch the laden barges towing past. Digging Burnet Street houses and shops out of the red silt would take days, but flood patrols, transformed into pump crews and salvage squads, went methodically to work pumping, shoveling, carting, and housewives laden with scrubbing brushes almost trod on their heels. The river front would carry the scars of the flood for many a long month, but they would be clean scars anyway.

Dirck roused early Wednesday morning. The sun was not even clear of the trees across the river, and sounds down on the towpath were only a murmur. Lazily content, he rolled over on his back, thrusting his hands comfortably under his head. There was no need to get up yet, and it was good to be in his own bed again, good to be home. They had mopped and pumped and scoured and scrubbed every spare moment. Mrs. Brandt and Maddy, once their own cellar was pumped out, had worked valiantly to help, charging into mud as if it were an enemy to be routed. Now even his mother was almost ready to admit the house was habitable again.

Today Mr. Sylvester would begin repairing damage to the partly finished shoring along the canal, and this afternoon Dr. Schureman would bring Pieter home. The strange interlude was over. By tomorrow he'd be back at the Queen himself. Idly, he wondered if Mr. Ten Eyck had got back to town. He'd been away in Trenton on canal business when they found the rubies in the clock, but Ann Augusta and Court Van Voorhees had come rowing down the very next day to thank them all.

That reminded him he hadn't had time to work on the clock case. After supper tonight he'd get it out and begin. Mrs. Brandt thought it was hopeless after the ducking Heinie gave it, but a little sandpaper and oil and a lot of elbow grease would surprise her. Suddenly it occurred to him that he could get the barn loft all cleaned up over there before Maddy came out to scrub the steps if he got straight up. Not having any garden left to tend gave him lots of time, and he owed Maddy that clean-up after the way she had worked at his house. He climbed into his clothes and ran quietly down the stairs and out to the path.

The ground felt marshy under his feet, and a reddish-brown coat of mud covered the meadows stretching down to the outlet. The purple vetch and the orange paintbrushes Maddy loved to see had been sponged away overnight by the flood. Only along the high slopes on Sonoman's Hill where chickory bloomed, blue and misty in the distance, were any wild flowers left. People claimed that chickory in bloom meant summer was nearly over. Soon new classes would begin at Rutgers; new students would come trooping into town.

Dirck gave himself a mental shaking. Why couldn't he forget once in awhile? When your dreams were just water over the dam, it was silly to remember them. The time had come to get down to earth. Darting into the Brandt barn, he climbed up to the loft and began to sweep as furiously as if he were trying to brush the dreams out of his own head.

Maddy, coming along later to feed her hens, caught him hard at it. Roosting at the top of the ladder, she watched silently, her eyes dancing, until he happened to turn around and spot her.

"Don't let me stop you," she said. "There was so much flapping going on in here, I just thought I'd investigate. How'd I know the chickens hadn't moved back in when I wasn't looking?"

Dirck shook a mop out of the window.

"How long you been sitting there?" he demanded. "For a girl who wasn't going to wait around for me to help clean up, you're doing mighty well."

Maddy dimpled. "I didn't want to clean this place one bit," she admitted. She stepped out into the loft and inspected his handiwork. "You did it very well indeed, Mr. Van Arsdalen," she said judicially. "I do believe you'll turn out to be right useful yet."

Dirck shook his head sadly. "Too bad I can't say the same about you," he told her.

Maddy's retort was cut short by the croak of a horn outside. "Mercy on us, Dirck Van Arsdalen, there goes your mother's breakfast horn, and I haven't even fed those chickens. You fly out of here right away."

She picked up her bag of corn and backed down the ladder in a hurry. Dirck followed as far as the side path.

"Come on over and see Pieter later," he suggested. "He'll be home today."

Maddy nodded. "I'll be over before supper," she called and sped across the yard to her waiting hens.

All morning the Van Arsdalen house hummed with activity. Running in and out on errands from the outlet, Dirck heard his mother singing in the kitchen, her mixing spoon merrily beating time. Spicy whiffs lured him to the cooky jar so often that she threatened to hook the back door, but by dinnertime, in spite of his raids, it looked as though the household could feed a regiment and have plenty left over for tomorrow. Even Mrs. Van Arsdalen was satisfied. Her visible approval of her morning's output drew chuckles from her husband and son.

"Go ahead and laugh," she said gaily. "This is the first time I've felt normal since the flood started, and I don't mind a bit."

But dinner dishes washed up, Mrs. Van Arsdalen was glad to rest in the shade of the maples by the front door and wait quietly for Dr. Schureman's carriage to turn down their lane. The clop of the horses' hoofs fetched Mr. Van Arsdalen and Dirck on the run.

Supported by his brother's strong young shoulder, Pieter walked slowly into the kitchen and settled in the chair ready for him by the back window. He was thin and feeble, but his eyes had their old twinkle, and his voice was surprisingly strong.

"Best keep him on this floor," Dr. Schureman advised

them. "No use struggling with stairs. Fix him up in the front room where he can avoid visitors when he's tired." He turned to Pieter. "I'll see you again, young fellow. Feels good to be home, eh?"

Mrs. Van Arsdalen's eyes followed him gratefully as he bustled out. Then she tackled the problem of settling Pieter downstairs. Maddy, flying in a moment later, made up the bed Dirck brought down and plumped the cushions in the armchair nearby before his father carried Pieter in to his temporary quarters.

"I'll rest awhile," he promised dutifully, "but don't either of you young'uns run away. With a pair of heroes in the house, I don't intend to be cheated out of their adventures; I want the whole story."

"We'll hang around," Dirck assured him, "so be ready to have your hair stand on end when we come back."

Closing the door carefully, they trooped into the kitchen to rejoice over Pieter's return. Dirck and his father moved reluctantly toward the back porch.

"Pieter's tired enough to sleep quite awhile," Mrs. Van Arsdalen consoled them. "We'll call you when he wakes. And, Dirck, run over to Brandts's and tell Maddy's mother we're keeping her for supper."

The boy was pleased. "I'll go right away. You can turn Maddy into a nurse for Pieter."

Maddy laughed at him. "Imagine your mother parting with that job! I'll be cook."

Her face glowing, she watched from the doorway as Dirck started across the fields.

"He cleaned up the barn loft for me this morning," she

told Mrs. Van Arsdalen. "I owe him a good supper."

"So that's how he got the cobwebs in his hair." His mother smiled as she tied an apron around Maddy's waist. "I wondered what he'd been crawling through when he came in to breakfast. Vegetable hash and rolls and pie for supper, Maddy. Any suggestions?"

"Shall I bake the hash in ramekins and make a cheese sauce?"

At a prompt nod, she settled competently to business, her flying fingers making short work of chopping vegetables and packing them into the buttered molds. Mrs. Van Arsdalen watched with interest; Maddy had a knack for avoiding waste motions. Sensing the older woman's scrutiny, the girl looked up a bit anxious, but Mrs. Van Arsdalen was smiling. "You'll make a good housekeeper, Maddy," she said quietly.

The girl flushed guiltily at the praise. "I'm not a bit like you and Mother," she confessed honestly. "You feel safe and comfortable in a house, but I just feel cooped up. Mother loves to stay in one place. She feels lost without her own stove. But every time I see a boat, I want to sail away."

"Your mother and I are like house cats, Maddy; we love a permanent hearthstone. But there's nothing wrong with the way you feel." Mrs. Van Arsdalen's kind voice was reassuring. "Women like you helped build towns in the wilderness and traveled west in covered wagons—and were good housekeepers while they were doing it. My gracious, they had to be, to make homes wherever they happened to light for a spell."

She laughed a little. "Don't expect us house cats to understand you; we never will. Just the same I still think you'll be a good housekeeper, even if you live in a tent."

Maddy's spirits promptly bounced back to normal. "As long as you don't think it's queer, I don't mind any more," she exclaimed.

CHAPTER TWENTY

Winner Take All

SUPPER WAS PREPARED and a tray ready to carry in to Pieter by the time he woke, rested and hungry. While his mother was helping him into his armchair, Maddy blew the supper horn and inspected the table critically. The hungry way Dirck sniffed when he smelled the ramekins, she guessed he'd like her cooking this time anyway.

Gathered around the table, they kept the door to the front room open to include Pieter in the family circle and see he had everything he wanted. They ate in such a festive mood that nobody wanted to hurry. Everyday things like washing dishes seemed not to matter at all, as they lingered to give Pieter installments of all the events he had missed, but Mrs. Van Arsdalen and Maddy exchanged guilty looks, caught unready, when Mr. Sylvester's hearty hail sounded from the back path. He stuck a smiling face through the kitchen door.

"You look too comfortable to be disturbed," he said, "but I'm coming in anyway."

They welcomed him heartily. Dirck, eager to learn how extensive the flood damage had been along the canal shoring, was ready with questions, but the engineer spied Pieter in the next room and strolled in to exchange greetings. Back again in the kitchen, he put a small parcel he'd been carrying down on the table and settled to the rolls and chocolate Maddy served him. No, things weren't too bad on the construction job; washouts, of course, where they hadn't had time to finish shoring before the river rose; nothing though that a little time couldn't remedy.

They were still talking of the engineer's work when the crunch of wheels in the lane, followed by quick steps along the side of the house, warned them of another visitor. This time it was Nicholas Ten Eyck, but he wouldn't sit down until he'd wrung Dirck's hand and thanked Maddy.

"My daughter and Court Van Voorhees poured the story into my ears the minute I stepped back into town. Since then Mr. Sylvester and Marshall Fitten have added the official version. It's difficult to express my gratitude to you young people adequately."

He smiled down at Margaretta Van Arsdalen. "You and Mrs. Brandt have reason to be proud of their courage and resourcefulness."

Dirck and Maddy flushed with pleasure at the warm sincerity in his voice.

"It was mostly luck, though, wasn't it, Maddy?" the boy said. "Were you surprised, sir, that the thief turned out to be Mr. Farquhar? Maybe if it hadn't rained so long and kept him holed up at the Queen, he'd have got clean away. Still, Mr. Farquhar wasn't so smart really, not when he picked a confederate like Heinie!"

Mr. Ten Eyck laughed. "He'll have plenty of time to

wish he'd chosen more wisely. His sentence will hardly be a light one."

He sat down and turned to the engineer, his eyebrows arched in a question. Guy Sylvester nodded. Taking his pipe out of his mouth, he said quietly, "Go ahead, Nicholas; I can chime in later."

Mr. Ten Eyck drew his chair a bit closer to the table and began to talk, his gaze fixed on Dirck and Mr. Van Arsdalen seated side by side.

"Suppose you hear me out, sir," he addressed the lock-keeper. "Then we can thresh out any questions you want to raise."

Considerably puzzled, Mr. Van Arsdalen agreed, waiting patiently for Mr. Ten Eyck to explain.

"Let me say first that I am speaking for Arent Coejemann as well as myself, Van Arsdalen," Mr. Ten Eyck said. "He's as enthusiastically behind this idea as Guy Sylvester and I. Perhaps you remember that a reward for the recovery of the rubies has been cried again and again. That reward, of course, belongs to Maddy and Tinker."

He held up his hand peremptorily at their startled exclamations.

"Mr. Coejemann didn't have time to offer a reward, but his desire to express his appreciation in some tangible form is no less keen than mine. In fact, he came to me about the matter as soon as I returned to town, and we talked it over together. Guy Sylvester came into our conferences as consultant. I assure you I am speaking for us all when I say we earnestly hope you will approve our plan. It is the result of much sober thought. In brief, sir, we should like to give the entire cash reward to Maddy Brandt, and for Tinker's share instead, send him to Rutgers for two years, beginning this September."

Before the astounded listeners could speak, Guy Sylvester's decisive voice had picked up where Mr. Ten Eyck stopped.

"We're not setting the boy to chasing will-o'-the-wisps, Van Arsdalen," he said firmly. "This proposition is practical. I've watched Tinker all summer. There's no question that he has the makings of an engineer. An apprenticeship with Sylvester and Simcoe is waiting for him at the end of those two years."

Dirck's face went white, and the room spun like a top around him. He couldn't speak, but his eyes clung to his father. The lockkeeper, however, sat like a man of wood, his mind struggling to grasp the implications of all Mr. Ten Eyck and Mr. Sylvester had said. Across the table Mrs. Van Arsdalen and Maddy, their eyes starry, watched him appealingly. Disturbed, his independence up in arms, Mr. Van Arsdalen had started to turn to his wife when Pieter spoke urgently from the front room.

"Dirck earned this reward, Father. Let him go to Rutgers. Didn't you really know why he went to work at the Queen? Did you think I hadn't guessed he was going to give up his own plans to save mine? Why, we can pay Mr. Ten Eyck back, Father, Dirck and I together. Don't let pride stand in his way."

Mrs. Van Arsdalen's face was radiant with satisfaction in her sons.

"Listen to Pieter, Jacobus," she said quietly. "We have no right to stand in Dirck's way."

The lockkeeper squared his shoulders. "They're all on your side, Mr. Ten Eyck. Don't think me ungrateful for hesitating, sir. It's a more than generous offer you're making. If this is what the lad wants for himself, he shall have it. Let the decision be his."

Studying Dirck's face, he smiled abruptly. There was no need for the boy to speak. Mr. Van Arsdalen held out his hand to Mr. Ten Eyck.

"Thank you, sir," he said soberly. "We accept your offer as gladly as you made it."

Pieter's delighted whoop roused Dirck from his speechless excitement. Maddy was already trying to express her thanks. Now, flushed and happy, he stammered out his own gratitude, but the men waved it aside.

"Nonsense, Tinker," Mr. Ten Eyck said. "We're hardheaded businessmen, Mr. Coejemann and I, and we think we're making a good investment. As for Guy over there," his eyes twinkled; "he comes out on top of the heap; he gets another apprentice to set to hard labor."

He made his farewells shortly, after planning to confer with Mr. Van Arsdalen in a day or two to settle details.

"Coming along, Guy?" he asked. "We've kept Mrs. Van Arsdalen from finishing her work long enough."

"Right you are, Nicholas," the engineer said. He reached over and picked up the parcel on the table. "I nearly forgot Staats Barckaloe's message." Grinning, he turned to Dirck. "He sent this along to you, Tinker; said you had the rest of it and might as well have it all as a souvenir." Still chuckling, he followed Mr. Ten Eyck out to his carriage in the lane.

Puzzled, Dirck turned the package over, but Maddy was in no mood to wait.

"Open it, Dirck," she said excitedly. "Don't be such a poke."

Standing at his elbow, she watched while he tore off the wrappings and opened a cardboard box to find the works of the Queen's now famous clock neatly wrapped in one of Antje Molenaer's kitchen towels. Dirck roared with laughter. Happily he presented the box to his mother.

"For you," he said smiling. "It doesn't look like much right now, but just wait till I finish with it. You'll never have an excuse to be late with dinner again!"

"I'll take your word for it," Mrs. Van Arsdalen said, smiling back at him; "but right now I don't need a clock to tell me how late it's getting. You walk Maddy home this minute, or Mrs. Brandt will never let us borrow her again. No," she silenced the girl's protest, "I don't need a bit of help with these dishes. I'm going to do them myself just to make sure I'm not dreaming."

Standing on tiptoe, she gave her tall son a hug and waved them down the path. Now that Pieter was getting well and Dirck's dream had turned into reality, she had nothing left to ask. Dirck's wages would still keep Pieter in the seminary; working nights wouldn't hurt him a bit. It was good for them to help each other. Pouring water into the dishpan, she began to sing softly to herself.

Wandering along the path, Dirck and Maddy lost all track of time. How could they hurry when the whole future had to be mapped in a stroll across a meadow? Excited and eager, their voices planned confidently ahead.

"Oh, Dirck, you'll build bridges in jungles and mountains; maybe someday you'll build a canal yourself!"

Maddy's face was a marvel of delight.

Dirck nodded. "I'll build them, Maddy," his voice rang with happiness; "but you'll come watch. Promise, Maddy. Sure!"

Author's Note

For the information of local historians I willingly confess that I have felt free to retain some thoroughly picturesque names that had been replaced by 1854. For example, by that time the Indian Queen Tavern had been renamed The Bell; the *Antelope* had shortly before sailed for San Francisco; and The Napoleon Company had been liquidated, and followed by companies with such unimaginative names as The Camden and Amboy Railroad and Transportation Company.

I want also to take this opportunity to thank Mr. Donald Cameron and Mr. Kenneth Q. Jennings, both of Rutgers University, for their friendly help in locating material I needed.